DARKENING SKIES

Darkening Skies

LEFT BEHIND®

>THE KIDS<

Jerry B. Jenkins

Tim LaHaye

WITH CHRIS FABRY

TYNDALE HOUSE PUBLISHERS, INC.
WHEATON, ILLINOIS

Visit Tyndale's exciting Web site at www.tyndale.com

Discover the latest Left Behind news at www.leftbehind.com

Published in association with the literary agency of Alive Communications, Inc., 7680 Goddard Street, Suite 200, Colorado Springs, CO 80920.

Edited by Curtis H. C. Lundgren

ISBN 0-8423-4312-1

Printed in the United States of America

08   07   06   05   04   03   02   01

9   8   7   6   5   4   3   2   1

To Scott

TABLE OF CONTENTS

About the Authors

What's Gone On Before

JUDD Thompson Jr. and Lionel Washington are in Israel with their friend Mr. Stein. As they drink in the teaching at the Meeting of the Witnesses, Judd spies Taylor Graham about to shoot down Nicolae Carpathia's helicopter. Taylor is stopped at the last minute, but Judd feels he must tell a Global Community security guard about Taylor to protect the witnesses.

Vicki and the others at the old schoolhouse discover an underground tunnel that leads to the river. The surviving Morale Monitor, Melinda, tells Vicki her story. Vicki prays that the girl will stay and hear more about God.

Mark decides to leave the kids and return to Mount Prospect to check on his aunt. As the others watch coverage of the meeting in Israel, they receive a strange E-mail. Someone at a Global Community outpost is trying to get in touch with Mark.

When the Meeting of the Witnesses ends, Judd sees Buck Williams run across the stage. A security guard shoots at him. When Judd reaches the guard, he notices the man has the mark of the true believer on his forehead. Suddenly, more shots ring out. Judd and Lionel dive for cover. The security guard is hit and dies in Judd's arms.

Vicki discovers Melinda is missing. Now, the Young Trib Force must pull together as danger increases around them.

ONE

Under the Stage

JUDD gently lowered the guard to the ground, knowing the man had died trying to protect Buck Williams and the others in the Tribulation Force. Footsteps pounded on the stage above them.

Lionel grabbed the guard's walkie-talkie. "Come on, we have to get out of here!"

Judd and Lionel rolled under the stage and held their breath. The radio squawked in Lionel's hand. He turned it down.

Two guards jumped from the stage and felt for a pulse on the downed guard. One barked into his radio, "He's dead, sir."

A voice shot back, "Find the rabbi and those others. I want them dead before they get out of the stadium!"

Judd whispered to Lionel, "We've got to stop them!"

But before Judd could move, another voice blared on the guard's radio. "We've spotted them in a Mercedes a few blocks from the stadium, sir."

"Probably headed to the Rosenzweig estate," another voice said. "After them!"

Judd sighed. "Nothing we can do now."

The stadium was nearly empty. A few stragglers knelt near the stage, praying. Medical personnel attended to the injured.

Judd and Lionel watched from the shadows as GC peacekeepers dragged the dead guard away. A cameraman flipped on a light, and a reporter stepped in front of it. "We are live at Teddy Kollek Stadium," the reporter said. "Just moments ago, this Global Community peacekeeper was murdered at the conference called the Meeting of the Witnesses. Those in the audience listened to a message of love and peace, but it seems someone did not follow their leader's teaching."

"No way one of the witnesses shot that guard," Lionel said.

Judd gritted his teeth. "Carpathia will make Tsion look—"

"What?" Lionel said.

Judd spied a heavyset boy near the front row. "I know that kid," he said.

When the Global Community guards were

gone, Judd and Lionel crept from under the stage and approached the boy.

The boy's mouth dropped open. "Judd," the boy said, "what are you doing here?"

"How do I know you?" Judd said.

"I'm Samuel. Nina and Dan Ben-Judah were my neighbors." Samuel had given Judd the video of the murders of Tsion's family.

"I wondered what happened to you," Judd said. "They took the video you gave me and—"

"We should not stay here," Samuel interrupted. "Come with me."

"We have to find our friend," Lionel said.

"You can find him later," Samuel said. "The followers of the rabbi are in danger. Come to my house."

Judd told Samuel their things were at the university. Samuel said, "We will go there on the way. Quickly! My father must not see you."

"Why not?" Judd said.

"He is working with the Global Community!"

Vicki ran to the others to tell them about Melinda. Phoenix ran beside her, clearly glad to be free from the rope and tape Melinda had wrapped around his legs. When Vicki entered, Darrion held up a hand.

"Just a minute," Vicki said, "I need to talk to you all."

"But something terrible's happened!" Darrion said.

Vicki yelled. "Please! Melinda's gone! She tied Phoenix up and left."

Conrad said, "How long ago?"

"I can't tell," Vicki said. "Let's search the house and the woods."

"I'll check the shed for the motorcycle," Conrad said.

"Sorry, Darrion," Vicki said, "but this is important."

Darrion hung her head. "I thought you'd be concerned about Judd and Lionel and Mr. Stein."

"What do you mean?"

"Shots were fired at the stadium."

Vicki put a hand over her mouth. "The GC is shooting at the witnesses?"

Darrion shook. "I'm scared, Vick."

"Judd and Lionel can take care of themselves," Vicki said, hugging Darrion.

The kids found no trace of Melinda in the house. Conrad said, "At least she didn't take the last motorcycle. She has to be on foot."

Vicki looked at her watch. "Plenty of daylight left, but we have to spread out."

Conrad and Darrion roared off on the motorcycle toward the main road. The others split up on foot. Vicki prayed as she ran into the woods.

GC emergency vehicles stopped traffic as Judd walked with Lionel and Samuel to the university. Lionel turned up the walkie-talkie and heard peacekeepers relaying information.

"They must be checking every car," Judd said.

"The GC are very upset about the rabbi and what he has done," Samuel said.

Judd turned. "Why are you helping us? You're not a follower of Dr. Ben-Judah."

"How do you know?" Samuel said.

Judd glanced at Lionel. "We can tell."

"Nina and Dan were my friends," Samuel said. "I feel terrible about what happened to them. I would not want to see the same thing happen to you."

Hundreds of witnesses gathered outside the gymnasium. A commotion at the front caught Judd's attention. GC guards led a dozen people from the building.

"What's going on?" Judd asked a man nearby.

"They are arresting the local committee," the man said.

Yitzhak Weizmann, the man who had given them shelter before the meetings began, was being led away in handcuffs. Behind him stood other committee members, including the meeting emcee.

The man next to Judd said, "They suspect the group is hiding the rabbi."

Judd gasped. The last man out the door was Mr. Stein. Judd shouted and waved and pushed his way to the front, but a uniformed officer appeared at the door with a bullhorn. "Attention, everyone who was using this gymnasium for shelter!" The officer passed the bullhorn to another man, who repeated his statement in several different languages.

"This is a crime scene," the man continued. "We have your belongings, and we will keep them until this situation is resolved."

"Mr. Stein's money!" Lionel whispered. "That's the only way we're getting home."

"Form a single line to register for your belongings," the officer said.

People lined up, but Samuel pulled Judd and Lionel away. "Do not give them your names. Come with me."

"We have to help Mr. Stein," Judd said.

"I can help you get him out," Samuel said, "but you must come with me."

Judd and Lionel followed Samuel back into the traffic near the stadium. They got in a cab, but the driver yelled at Samuel in Hebrew, and the three retreated.

"What did he say?" Judd said.

"He cursed at us," Samuel said. "Because of the traffic, he cannot move."

They walked through the congested streets. "You have heard about the meeting at the Wailing Wall tomorrow?" Samuel said.

"We'll be there," Judd said.

"Don't," Samuel said. "The GC are planning to execute Dr. Ben-Judah."

"Carpathia promised he wasn't going to hurt anybody," Lionel said.

"They're going to make it look like a terrorist attack," Samuel said.

"You know this because of your father?" Judd said.

Samuel nodded.

"Why did he let you go to that meeting?" Lionel said.

"He didn't know," Samuel said. "I came on my own."

They passed a crowded bar, and a photo of the guard Judd had met flashed on a big-screen television inside. Beneath his photo were the years of his birth and death.

"Wish I could hear this," Judd said.

"We're not far from my house," Samuel said. "We can watch there."

Lionel pulled Judd aside. "His father's working with the GC!"

"He trusted me with the videotape. He's okay. He wants to help."

"But he doesn't have the mark."

"Maybe we can change that," Judd said.

Conrad and Darrion returned and met Vicki and the others near the shed to discover that still no one had seen Melinda.

"I say we head toward town," Darrion said.

Vicki's weird friend Charlie walked up. "What are you guys going to do with her after you catch her?"

Vicki looked at the others and shrugged. "Drag her back here?"

Conrad scratched his chin. "I don't care. I just want to find her."

"Maybe she doesn't want to rat us out," Vicki said. "Maybe she just wants to get away."

Shelly agreed. "Tsion's message could have been too much for her. She might just need time."

"And she might run into the GC," Conrad

said, "which would be the end for her. Let me at least stay on the road awhile."

Judd and Lionel crept to the back door of Samuel's house and followed him in. Emergency vehicles screamed by, sirens blaring. Samuel answered the ringing phone. "My father," he mouthed.

"Did he tell you what's happening?" Judd said as Samuel hung up.

"He told me to stay inside. The crazy zealots are killing people."

Samuel turned on the television, and the photo of the guard flashed on the screen again. Another photo appeared beside the guard.

"It's Buck!" Lionel shouted.

The news anchor looked grim. "Global Community forces believe this videotape reveals this man as the murderer at Teddy Kollek Stadium. The suspect has been identified as American Cameron Williams, former employee of the GC publishing division. Williams is reportedly staying with Rabbi Tsion Ben-Judah at the home of Israeli Nobel Prize–winner Dr. Chaim Rosenzweig."

Lionel's radio squawked. "Proceeding to the Rosenzweig estate," a man said.

"That is only a few blocks from here," Samuel said.

Leon Fortunato, Nicolae Carpathia's right-hand man, appeared on the screen at a news conference. "We will do what we must to bring these criminals to justice. We have witnesses to the act, a videotape recording, and several of the local committee members in custody. Rest assured, we will bring to justice the man or woman who did this."

"Buck was running away when the guard was shot," Lionel said. "The videotape has to show that."

"The truth never stops these people," Judd said.

Samuel brought snacks, and Judd and Lionel ate as they watched the news and monitored the guard's radio.

"Has your dad always worked for the GC?" Lionel said.

Samuel shook his head. "Only since the murder of Dr. Ben-Judah's family. My father had helped them in the past, but that changed when the rabbi abandoned his faith. My father went totally for the Global Community and Nicolae Carpathia. He works—"

A roar went over the house. Judd ran to the window and saw a brilliant flash.

"A GC chopper," Samuel said.

"Closing in on Buck and Tsion, I bet," Judd said. "We have to help."

"You can't go there," Samuel said.

"These are our friends," Judd said. "We might be able to do something."

Samuel told them how to find the Rosenzweig estate, then turned on a light at the rear of the house. "If this light is off when you return, tap on my window and I'll let you in."

The night air was cool and the streets almost deserted. Judd and Lionel rounded a corner and saw two squad cars parked in front of a huge gate. They could hear the chopper nearby.

Lionel listened to the banter of the GC peacekeepers on the walkie-talkie. Chaim Rosenzweig wasn't letting them inside.

The chopper hovered over the estate, then put down on top of the house.

"They're going in through the roof," Lionel said.

Judd peered through the darkness at the GC insignia on the side of the chopper. Three figures leaped into the helicopter just before it lifted off and headed north, a few feet above the rooftops.

Another chopper approached from the south and hovered directly over them. The frantic voice of the pilot came over the radio, trying to communicate with the other chopper.

"Tsion and Buck have to be in the first chopper," Judd said.

"Who else was with them?" Lionel said. "Chloe?"

Judd shrugged. "Let's head back to Samuel's house before they spot us."

Just after 1 A.M. Judd and Lionel found the light off. Judd tapped lightly on Samuel's window. A light came on over the door. Judd and Lionel climbed the steps and waited.

Something moved behind them.

Samuel opened the door and smiled. "I knew it! I told you they'd come back!"

Judd turned. A man stood behind them, holding a gun. "Good work, Son."

TWO

Samuel's Deception

"YOU LIED!" Judd said as the man shoved him and Lionel inside. Samuel led them to two chairs in the living room.

"You were trying to help Ben-Judah escape," Samuel said. "Doesn't matter what I did to catch you."

"He won't escape," Samuel's father said.

"You can't hold us here," Judd said. "We didn't do anything."

"Shut up," Samuel's father said. He turned to his son. "How'd you find them?"

"You know I felt guilty about shooting that video. Then, when it was stolen—"

"Stolen?" Judd said.

"Be quiet!" Samuel's father said.

"Tonight I went to the meeting to see if I could expose some of the zealots." Samuel glared at Judd. "They preach hatred. They think their way is the only way. Then I saw Judd, the very one who had taken the video. I knew if I could get him to come back here, you would know what to do."

"I told you to stay away from the stadium," Samuel's father said. "You could have been killed." The man sighed. "But finding these Americans might help us."

"They knew some of the men arrested at the university tonight," Samuel said. "And they are friends with Ben-Judah and the others staying with Rosenzweig."

Judd said, "So the potentate was lying when he promised protection for the witnesses?"

"Carpathia does not lie," Samuel's father said. "You saw what the zealots did to him and the supreme pontiff. They were completely—"

"I was there," Judd said. "Why are you working with the GC? Were you afraid they'd find out you helped Ben-Judah's family?"

"How did you know—"

"Your son told me before he gave me the video of the murders," Judd said.

"I did not!" Samuel shouted. "I tried to help you, and you repay me by stealing?"

"The question is how much you know," Samuel's father said, "and whether you can help us capture the fugitives."

"Never," Lionel said, "even if we knew where they were."

The phone rang. Samuel's father handed his gun to Samuel and hurried into the next room to answer it. "This is Goldberg," Judd heard him say. "I had to leave . . . no, I did not realize that, sir . . . how many?"

Samuel turned on the television to more reports of the killing at the stadium. Finally, Mr. Goldberg returned.

"Your friends are gone," he said. "They stole a Global Community helicopter and flew to Jerusalem Airport. All of them escaped onto a plane except one. He's dead."

The phone rang again.

"Who's dead?" Lionel said.

Judd shook his head. "He might be lying."

Samuel turned up the television. Lionel whispered, "My ID says I'm Greg Butler, but if they find out I'm a Morale Monitor . . ."

"Did they fingerprint you?" Judd said.

"Yeah," Lionel said. "And they printed you when you and Taylor Graham were arrested, right?"

Judd sighed. "Our IDs won't do us any good if they check the prints. We have to get out of here."

From the next room Judd heard Mr. Goldberg say, "I may have more answers after I question these two."

Samuel glanced at Judd and moved toward the door. "What's the matter, Father?"

Judd rushed Samuel and knocked him to the ground, the gun clattering to the floor. Before Judd or Lionel could reach it, Mr. Goldberg ran in and grabbed it. "Stop!"

Judd flung open a door just as the gun went off. Wood splintered above his head as he and Lionel dove for cover.

Judd swung the door shut, leaving him and Lionel in darkness. The room smelled musty. Mr. Goldberg jiggled the doorknob and put his weight against the door.

"Good choice," Mr. Goldberg said, laughing. He locked the door from the outside. "That should keep you until the GC arrive."

Judd felt along the wall for a light switch. He flipped it on and saw that they were at the top of a landing. Stairs led to the basement.

"Find a way to block the door," Judd said.

"But they locked it from the other—"

"Just block the door. Hurry!"

Judd raced down the stairs and got his bearings. In one corner he found a large dresser. He pulled out the drawers and moved it away from the wall. Behind the dresser he found a doorway that had been nailed shut. He quickly located a toolbox and found a hammer.

Lionel came down the stairs, out of breath. "I did the best I could," he gasped. "How did you know about this door?"

"Dan and Nina led me through here once," Judd said.

Judd pried off the wood, trying not to be heard. He had two corners free when he heard a siren outside. "That's the GC," he said, and he and Lionel attacked the door. As they pried the last plank away, footsteps sounded overhead. Someone tried to open the door at the top of the stairs, then smashed it, splintering the wood. Judd felt the chill of the night air as he and Lionel pried open the secret door.

He threw the hammer and burst the lightbulb that lit the room. Someone yelled, "They've got a gun!"

Judd and Lionel rushed out into the night and nearly ran Samuel over. "I knew you'd find the passage," he whispered.

Judd braced for a fight. "Stay out of our way!"

Samuel slipped them a piece of paper. "Go to this address. They will take you in, no questions asked."

"What?" Lionel said. "No way we'll trust you."

"Go," Samuel said. "I will explain later."

They ran to a main street, where many of the witnesses still milled about. A helicopter passed, its light scanning the crowd. Judd and Lionel blended with the others. Judd read the address Samuel gave them.

"You're not—," Lionel said.

"What choice do we have?" Judd said.

Lionel sighed. "A hotel?"

"How much money do you have?" Judd said.

Lionel emptied his pockets. Not enough.

"The GC will check the hotels anyway," Judd said. He held up the paper to the light. "This is our only good option."

Judd asked for directions several times before they found the right street. As they moved farther from the Old City, fewer people passed them. Finally they were alone outside a tall apartment building. Judd rang the buzzer, but there was no answer. He rang again.

"We have company," Lionel said.

Judd glanced around. A Global Community squad car sat across the street.

"Let's run for it," Judd said. "You go to the right—"

But the door buzzed and they slipped

inside to find a dark elevator. Someone stood in the shadows. A gun clicked.

"Face forward," a man said.

He was short with dark hair, a large nose, and a mustache. He pointed the semiautomatic pistol at Judd. "I said face forward."

Judd turned. The man told him to punch the top button. The rickety elevator slowly climbed to the twelfth floor.

"Who sent you?" the man said.

"Samuel," Judd said. "Don't know his last name. He was friends—"

"Were you followed?" the man interrupted.

"Not that we know of," Lionel said. "But this GC squad car—"

"We saw," the man said. "A routine check. But your timing was not exactly perfect."

"Who's *we?*" Judd said.

The elevator opened. "To your right," the man said.

Judd and Lionel stepped onto faded brown carpet. The hallway was dark. Several sockets had no lights. At the end of the hall was a stairwell. "Keep going," the man said.

Judd and Lionel climbed the stairs to what looked like a janitor's room. The door opened, and they were greeted by a woman wearing a veil.

The large room they were in led to several

smaller rooms and a hallway that looked as if it ran the entire length of the building.

The man locked the door behind him. "Sit," he said.

Lionel and Judd sat on a shabby couch. Stuffing showed at the edges of the cushions. The woman left the room and quietly closed the door. She came back a moment later and whispered something to the man.

"There are people sleeping," the man said.

Judd sat forward. "Who are you, and where are we?"

The man turned on a lamp and leaned close. He pulled back his thick, black hair and showed them the sign of the believer on his forehead.

"Why didn't you tell us?" Judd said.

"I wanted to make sure you were not followed," the man said. "My wife just told me the squad car is gone. I am Jamal. I run the apartment complex."

"You're the manager?" Lionel said.

"I would love to claim that title, but I'm afraid janitor would be closer to the truth. I will explain more, but you must first tell me what kind of trouble you are in."

Judd told the man about the Meeting of the Witnesses and going to Samuel's house. "How does Samuel know you?" Judd said. "He's not a believer."

"I do not know," the man said. "Perhaps the Global Community has set a trap. It troubles me to think a GC employee's son has our information."

"Are there other believers here?" Judd said.

"We kept many of the witnesses here throughout the meetings," Jamal said. "As many as a hundred per night. Most of them are gone, but a few are leaving tomorrow."

"We had a friend taken by the GC," Lionel said. "Mr. Stein is our only way back to the States."

"They will likely question and release him, unless they uncover something," Jamal said. "Contacts will keep us informed."

Judd had more questions, but Jamal held up a hand. "It is almost dawn. You are safe. That is all you need to know right now."

Jamal showed them a room with four beds. "Sleep, and may God watch over you and your friends."

Mark's mind reeled as he drove through the old neighborhood. He wanted to tell his aunt about John's death and see if he could help her, but after tracking her through various GC emergency shelters, Mark discovered she had been transferred to the same furniture store, which had been converted to a makeshift hospital, where Ryan had died. The man at the front wouldn't let him through, but Mark found a back entrance and searched a filing cabinet filled with patients' names. He found his aunt's name on a list of patients. She had died four days earlier.

Mark found the morgue and asked to see his aunt's body. "I'm sorry, son," the attendant said, "but a person unclaimed for that long is cremated."

Mark drove back to his aunt's house. There, he watched the Meeting of the Witnesses on Judd's laptop. It was hard to concentrate. He felt guilty for not being with his aunt when she needed him.

Not knowing what to do next, Mark decided to visit Z at the gas station. Z fed Mark and gave him a place to sleep. They talked.

"You haven't always seen eye to eye with Judd and Vicki, have you?" Z said.

"They don't see eye to eye with each other."

"But you were hooked up with the militia," Z said.

"I should have listened to them," Mark said, "but this is different. I don't feel like I've got a place there."

Z nodded. "I've been reading in the Bible about Paul and Barnabas. They disagreed and had to separate, and there were bad feelings, I guess. But later they worked it out."

Mark tried to sleep but couldn't. He joined Z early the next morning to watch the coverage of the meeting in Israel. By Friday night he had made his decision.

"I'm going back to see if I can hash it out with them," Mark said.

Early Saturday morning Mark headed back to the schoolhouse. At 9:00 A.M. he wound through the small town near the access road. He noticed a GC security vehicle and several officers.

Mark rode as close as he could without drawing attention. Several townspeople stood watching.

"What's going on?" Mark said to an older man.

"They caught some girl," the man said. "Been talking on the radio for quite a while. They got her in the back of the squad car."

Mark rode past the officers and stole a glance at the car. The door was slightly open. Mark gasped. Melinda sat in the backseat, crying. Her hands were cuffed.

THREE

The Chase

MARK parked his cycle and walked past a few stores. He wondered if Melinda had told the peacekeepers about the Young Trib Force and their hideout. He studied shopwindows as he listened to the squawking radios.

"Still waiting for the fingerprint ID," one officer said.

"She sure looks like the photo," another said. "Wonder how she wound up here?"

Mark walked into a small grocery store and watched the GC officers through the window. He bought a pack of gum and asked the girl at the cash register what happened.

"She ran in here out of breath," the girl said. "Real dirty. Looked like she'd spent the night in the woods. I figured it was one of those women who escaped from the GC prison I've been hearing about on the news."

"There was a breakout?" Mark said.

"Yeah. One of those reeducation camps or whatever you call them. When that girl saw the squad car go by, she freaked. Hid behind one of the aisles back there. I went outside and flagged 'em down."

"You're pretty much a hero," Mark said.

The girl blushed. "I didn't do nothin'. Just figured she had to be guilty of something, the way she acted."

Mark thanked the girl and left. A small bell rang as he opened the door and the peace-keepers glanced at him. Mark walked the other way.

The radio squawked. "Here's the report," a man said. "We have a negative on the down-state facility. Your girl is MM-1215, Melinda Bentley." The man read off more information about Melinda. "You're instructed to interro-gate, then carry out GC order X-13."

The peacekeepers looked at each other. "Can you repeat that?"

"Interrogate and carry out an X-13. Over."

The peacekeeper sighed. "Ten four, we copy. Out."

Mark didn't know what an X-13 was, but it didn't sound good for Melinda. He turned the corner and walked his motorcycle closer. He wanted to hear the GC question Melinda.

"We know who you are," a peacekeeper said. "Who's been hiding you?"

"I was staying with some friends," Melinda said.

"Who?"

Her handcuffs clinked as Melinda pushed the hair from her eyes.

"I don't know their names."

"Where?"

Melinda shrugged. "Talking to you isn't going to do me any good. I know what's going to happen."

Mark darted into the grocery store and handed the girl behind the counter a large bill. "What's this for?" she said.

"You'll see," Mark said. He walked into the street and faced the squad car. The peacekeepers leaned against the open door. Mark got Melinda's attention and motioned for her to get out of the car. She seemed to understand. Mark returned to the cycle.

"I'm tired of sitting here," Melinda said.

"Answer our questions and we'll take you for a long walk," a peacekeeper said, chuckling.

"Let me at least stretch my legs," Melinda said. "Then I'll tell you anything you want to know."

As soon as she was out of the car, Mark

started the cycle. He grabbed a loose brick and pulled into the street. As the peacekeepers turned, he threw the brick through the front window of the store.

"Hey!" one of the peacekeepers shouted. Both moved toward Mark.

"It slipped," Mark yelled.

"We saw you! Now get off your bike!" the second peacekeeper said, unlocking his gun holster.

Melinda inched around to the other side of the squad car. Mark gunned the engine and raced past the peacekeepers, who shouted at him and drew their weapons. He barreled around the car, and Melinda jumped on behind him.

Mark shot down an alley as gunfire erupted.

"I can't hold on!" Melinda shouted.

"Put your hands over my head," Mark shouted.

With the cuffs still on, Melinda slipped her hands over Mark's head and worked them down to his waist.

"Did you tell them about us?" Mark shouted.

"No!"

The GC squad car's siren blared behind them.

"Hang on," Mark said. "This is going to be some chase!"

Judd awoke late in the afternoon in Israel. Jamal stood in the doorway. "You have a visitor."

Judd woke Lionel. From a tiny monitor mounted near the door Judd saw someone pushing the buzzer on the first floor.

"Do you know him?" Jamal said.

"That's Samuel," Judd said. "His dad works for the GC."

Jamal shook his head. "I cannot allow him here. It is too great a risk."

"If he's the one who sent us, why can't we trust him?" Judd said.

Jamal studied the screen as Lionel said, "Maybe it was their plan to let us escape Samuel's house. To find this place. They may want you more than they want us."

Judd had to admit it was a possibility. "Still, something tells me Samuel's okay."

"Can we get outside some other way and meet him on the street?" Lionel said.

"There is a way," Jamal said, "but I can't let you endanger the lives of those we are hiding."

"We'll get outside and follow him to make sure it's safe," Judd said.

Jamal handed Judd a key, then took them through a corridor to the freight elevator. "This comes out at the back of the building. Go to the bottom floor, the garage. You can walk around to the front from there, but I warn you, watch out for anyone who looks like they're with the Global Community. If they catch you, you must never tell them about this place."

The garage was dingy and dark. Judd and Lionel hid behind bushes as they approached the front. No one was at the door.

"Guess he gave up," Lionel said.

Judd glanced both ways. "Want to split up?"

"Let's stick together," Lionel said.

They ran north three blocks. Lionel grabbed Judd's arm. Samuel stood in a nearby phone booth. Judd and Lionel approached slowly and listened.

"Please pick up the phone," Samuel said. "I sent two people to you yesterday. I need to talk with them. Their names are Judd and Lionel. They think—"

Samuel turned and saw them. He hung up the phone. "I am so glad to see you. We must talk."

"Where's your dad?" Judd said.

"At work," Samuel said. "He let me stay home from school because of last night."

"Do you ever go to school?" Judd said skeptically.

"I know a café nearby," Samuel said.

Samuel led them to the café. The waiter seated them in a secluded spot inside. Judd and Lionel kept an eye on the street. "We're almost out of cash," Judd said as he glanced at the menu.

"Don't worry, I will pay for this," Samuel said.

"One more favor," Judd said. "Unbutton your shirt."

"What for?" Samuel said.

"Just do it," Judd said.

When Judd was sure Samuel was not wearing a bug, he relaxed a little. The waiter came with their food, and Lionel and Judd ate hungrily. Samuel described what had happened after the two had escaped.

"They questioned me for an hour," Samuel said. "They wanted to know everything I knew about you. I told them the truth about meeting you the first time, but I lied about the video. I'm sorry."

"Did they connect us with Mr. Stein?" Lionel said.

"That is why I risked coming here," Samuel

said. "I had to tell them enough so they would believe me. They have interrogated Mr. Stein about you."

"They're still holding him?" Judd said.

"I overheard my father's phone call. Mr. Stein admitted he knew you both, but would say nothing further. The GC have beaten him severely."

"They beat him?"

"He is still in custody, but you must not try to help him escape. They are expecting you. I will get word to you when he is released."

"We can't tell you about the place we're staying," Lionel said.

Samuel nodded. "But I must know how to get you if something should happen."

Judd worked out a code with Samuel to use when calling Jamal's apartment. If Mr. Stein was freed or if he needed Judd and Lionel, Samuel would leave a message in code.

"We also need to know who was killed last night at the airport," Judd said.

"My dad will know," Samuel said. "I don't think the information has been released to the media."

As they finished their meal, Samuel grew quiet. Judd still didn't know whether to trust him, but so far, his story checked out. "What's the matter?" Judd said.

"There's another reason I came to see you," Samuel said. "It's about the meeting last night and some things the rabbi said."

Mark didn't want the GC squad car to follow him to the hideout, so he backtracked to the expressway. Most of the highway still had large gaps in it from the earthquake. Cars poked along.

The squad car was close when they first made it to the highway, but Mark rode on the edge of the pavement and dodged the slower cars.

"Where are you going?" Melinda shouted over the noise of the bike and the honking cars around them.

"Just hang on," Mark said.

Suddenly, Mark veered left and into the median. The bike slid sideways, but Mark regained control. The squad car followed, mud flying into the air behind it. Mark shot over the median and across the oncoming cars on the other side of the highway. Melinda screamed. A semitrailer swerved to miss them and hit another car, sending it careening toward the squad car.

Mark slowed as they went over an embankment he had seen earlier in the day. He drove through the edge of a cornfield and onto a small, country road.

"Are they still following us?" Mark yelled.

Melinda glanced back. "Not yet. I think the truck's blocking them."

Mark pushed the bike to its limits, screaming around curves. Three miles later, he turned off the engine and coasted down a hill to a small stream. "This is where we get off," Mark said. "Hurry."

Melinda struggled to get her hands over Mark's head. "We'll get those cuffs off you when we get back to the schoolhouse," Mark said.

Mark pushed the motorcycle to a stream that ran under the road. They found a dry place under the bridge and waited.

Finally, Mark whispered, "Why'd you leave the group?"

Melinda explained that she had heard Tsion's message. Coupled with the clear lies of Nicolae Carpathia, it was too much for her. "I had to get away."

"You don't believe what Tsion says?" Mark said.

"He has to be right," Melinda said, "but after all I've staked my life on . . . it's hard."

Mark nodded. "You went straight to that little town?"

"I hid from Vicki and the GC during the

night," Melinda said. "They came pretty close a couple of times, but I got under some brush.

"This morning I made it as far as the town when I spotted those peacekeepers. I tried to play it cool, but the girl in the store ratted me out."

"What's an X-13?" Mark said.

Melinda pursed her lips. "That's the order to eliminate a prisoner."

"They were going to kill you?" Mark said.

"If you hadn't come along, they would have," Melinda said.

Cars passed overhead. Dust and debris fell from the bottom of the bridge. Mark stuck his head out and quickly returned. "GC squad cars," he said.

Judd and Lionel talked with Samuel about Tsion's message. Samuel wanted to know what the people were doing who came to the front of the stadium. Judd told him.

Lionel jumped in with questions about what Samuel believed about God. Judd was impressed with the way Lionel showed Samuel the truth about Jesus.

"The Bible shows us that Jesus is more than just a good teacher," Lionel said. "He's God."

Samuel glanced at his watch and gasped. "My father! He will be home soon."

"You shouldn't put off this decision," Lionel said.

"I will relay information when I can," Samuel said. "I must go."

Lionel handed Samuel a piece of paper. The boy took it, put money on the table, and quickly walked away.

"What was that?" Judd said.

"A verse I found that might make him think," Lionel said.

Judd wondered if they would ever see Samuel again.

FOUR

Tragic News

JUDD and Lionel told Jamal what had happened. Jamal winced when he heard they had met with Samuel in a public place. Jamal turned on a videotape from the GC network that showed Buck Williams talking to the guard who had been killed.

"The news has been running this to show that Mr. Williams is guilty," Jamal said.

"Buck's not even carrying a gun," Lionel said.

"Exactly," Jamal said. "After Buck leaves, the guard fires over his head. Then, the guard is hit."

"How could they say Buck killed him?" Judd said.

Jamal shook his head. "The Global Community will cover up the truth. I'm afraid of what might happen to Mr. Williams and the others. Especially since the pilot is dead."

"What?" Judd said. His heart raced. "Rayford Steele is dead?"

Mark and Melinda kept quiet as the squad cars passed again. Clouds rolled in and the light grew dim.

"How long did it take you to get to the town?" Mark whispered.

"I'm not sure," Melinda said. "I had to hide so many times. Maybe a couple of hours. Why?"

"We're going to have to ditch the motorcycle," Mark said. He glanced at her. "That's assuming you want to go back."

Melinda looked away. "You sure you want to risk being seen with me?"

Mark smiled. "I risked getting you out this morning, didn't I?"

"Why do you people keep helping me?" Melinda said.

Mark picked up a rock and tried to break the chain between the cuffs. "We can't leave the cycle here. It's too close to the school-house."

"What do we do?" Melinda said.

"Wait here until nightfall."

The two listened to the stillness of the countryside. An occasional car passed, but the GC had apparently moved their search. Finally, Melinda broke the silence. "Why did *you* leave the schoolhouse?"

Mark told her about his fight with Vicki and his search for his aunt. "I don't see eye to eye with everybody in the group," he said, "but they're all the family I have now."

Melinda stared at Mark. "I'm sorry about your aunt."

Judd put his face in his hands. He couldn't believe Rayford Steele had been killed. Jamal rewound the tape.

A news reporter dramatically walked the runway at Jerusalem Airport. "One of the American terrorists was shot and killed here," he said. "It happened late last night, after the final session of the so-called Meeting of the Witnesses." The reporter walked near a Global Community helicopter. "The daring escape included hijacking Potentate Carpathia's own helicopter."

"That's what we saw last night!" Lionel said.

Chaim Rosenzweig's estate flashed on the screen. "Dr. Rosenzweig had hosted Ben-

Judah, murder suspect Cameron Williams, and Williams's wife. According to Global Community Supreme Commander Leonardo Fortunato, the escape was well calculated."

A disgusted Leon Fortunato was shown at a press conference. "We were assured that the prisoners were under house arrest. Upon further investigation, we found a door to the roof clearly broken from the inside. This shows conclusively how the Americans escaped."

The reporter knelt on the runway, pointing at a red stain. "When the helicopter landed here, an American terrorist opened fire on GC forces nearby. A sniper killed terrorist Ken Ritz with a single shot to the head."

"Do you know this Ritz?" Jamal said.

Judd shook his head. "He must have been working with Buck and Tsion."

The reporter stood in front of the downed helicopter. "The other three fugitives—suspected murderer Cameron Williams, his wife, and Tsion Ben-Judah—have escaped and are at large internationally. It is assumed that Williams is an accomplished pilot."

"What?" Lionel said. "Buck's smart, but he's never flown a plane before in his life."

"Somebody else had to help them get away," Judd said.

The reporter concluded by showing photos of Ben-Judah and Buck Williams. "These men are considered armed and extremely dangerous. If you have any information about their whereabouts, please contact your nearest Global Community post."

Vicki and the others tried to stay busy throughout the day, but each sound, every crack of a twig made them nervous. Finally, Vicki called a meeting.

"I've been reading a lot in Philippians," Vicki said. "Paul was a prisoner and was writing to encourage a church he helped start." Vicki opened the Bible. "Toward the end he said, 'I have learned how to get along happily whether I have much or little. I know how to live on almost nothing or with everything. I have learned the secret of living in every situation, whether it is with a full stomach or empty, with plenty or little. For I can do everything with the help of Christ who gives me the strength I need.'"

Vicki closed her Bible. "He was content even in prison. God had a purpose for him wherever he was. It's the same with us. Maybe God wants us to stay here. Maybe he wants us in some GC jail so we can talk to the people there. Whatever the situation, we need to be content."

"So you're saying we shouldn't be nervous about Melinda?" Darrion said. "Well, I am nervous. I don't want the GC to come in here and arrest us."

"Neither do I," Vicki said, "and we need to do everything we can to keep them from finding us. But at some point we have to trust God to protect us."

"I see your point," Conrad said. "I think the best thing we can do right now is pray that Melinda will come to her senses and return."

The kids gathered in a circle and joined hands. Each took a turn praying that God would bring Melinda back, or at least keep her from the Global Community.

As night approached, the kids ate dinner together. Vicki and Darrion answered some of the messages that had come in after the Meeting of the Witnesses. Kids around the world still begged to know God.

Conrad volunteered to take the first watch. While he put Phoenix on a chain in the front yard, Vicki gathered some blankets. Conrad climbed a narrow staircase that led to the old bell tower. As he settled in for the night, Vicki and the others tried to sleep.

Mark worked on Melinda's handcuffs throughout the day with several rocks he found by the stream. When one broke, he picked up another. Mark had rubbed blisters on his hands trying to break the cuffs. Once he missed and hit Melinda's wrist.

The chain between the two cuffs was nearly broken when something moved nearby. Mark looked at Melinda. He could barely see her face in the dim light. He put a finger to his lips and cautiously moved from his hiding place under the bridge.

As he stuck his head out, someone jumped into the water nearby. "I found you!" a girl shouted and nearly knocked Mark into the water. "I've heard that knocking sound all day."

The girl peered under the bridge and spotted Melinda. "Why's she got handcuffs on?"

Mark ignored her. "Who are you?"

"You first," the girl said.

Mark noticed the girl was wearing a jumpsuit that looked like it had come from a prison. But he couldn't keep from studying her face, which looked somehow familiar.

"Those are GC clothes," Melinda said.

The girl scowled. "I've been staying with

my uncle on his farm for a few days. He gave me these."

Finally, Mark remembered. "Janie!"

"How'd you know my name?" Janie shouted.

"You were being held at the GC reeducation camp," Mark said. "What are you doing out here?"

"A few of us got out last night," Janie said. "I got separated this morning. Then I saw all those GC cars. Decided I'd stay put until tonight." Janie eyed the motorcycle. "Is that yours?"

Mark nodded.

"Let me have it, and I won't tell anybody you're down here," Janie said.

"You won't get very far—," Melinda said, but Mark interrupted her.

"We were going to leave on foot anyway," Mark said. "You headed to Chicago?"

Janie nodded. "I got some friends back there who might help me."

Mark handed her the keys to the cycle. Janie turned. "You look familiar to me, too. How do I know you?"

"I went to Nicolae High," Mark said. "You were staying with a girl I knew."

"Vicki?" Janie said.

Mark nodded.

"She's the one I'm looking for," Janie said.

"Best friend I ever had. I've changed a lot since I last saw her."

"How?" Mark said.

"I've gotten more religious," Janie said. "You know where I can find her?"

Mark strained to see Janie's forehead, but couldn't. He wasn't sure Janie could be trusted. She had lied about staying with her uncle, but he might have done the same thing talking to strangers. He was going to let her take the cycle and lead the GC away from their hideout, but since she was looking for Vicki, he felt guilty letting her go.

"I can take you where she is," Mark said, "but we'll have to ditch the cycle." Mark explained their run-in with the GC and that Melinda was wanted by the GC as well.

"I hate to lose good wheels," Janie said, "but if you can help me find Vicki, let's go."'

Mark rolled the motorcycle to a hill near a lake and pushed it over the edge. The cycle splashed into the water and disappeared. The kids stole into the night, staying close enough to follow the road, then hiding when a car passed.

In the distance they saw the lights of the small town. Dogs barked. A squad car drove by on the interstate, its lights flashing. Mark

motioned for the girls to follow as they
entered the woods.

Judd and Lionel had slept so late in the day
that they couldn't get to sleep that night.
They sat in their room talking about Mr.
Stein and wondering what had happened.

They had eaten dinner with several other
witnesses and heard their fantastic stories of
how God had convinced them that Jesus was
the Messiah of the Jewish people. They talked
about the Meeting of the Witnesses, how
encouraging it had been, and what a fool
Nicolae Carpathia had made of himself.

When Judd explained about Mr. Stein,
several of the witnesses gathered to pray.
Others came from the nearby rooms, and
soon people were praying in different
languages for Mr. Stein's safety.

Later, while Judd and Lionel went over the
day's events, a beautiful girl with dark skin
and brown eyes knocked on their door and
entered. "Are you Judd?" she said.

Judd nodded.

"There is a phone call for you."

Judd went into the next room and found
Jamal and his wife. Jamal looked sternly at

Judd. "I do not like calls in the middle of the night."

Judd nodded and picked up the phone. It was Samuel.

"I called as quickly as I could," Samuel said, out of breath.

"What's wrong?" Judd said.

"Your friend, Mr. Stein," Samuel said. "Something has happened. I think he may have been released."

"Where can we find him?" Judd said.

"I don't know," Samuel said. "My father rushed from the house, very upset. I came to this pay phone immediately."

Judd thanked Samuel and told Jamal what had happened.

"Tomorrow I will call my contacts about him," Jamal said. "Get some rest."

Judd nodded. As he closed the door he noticed the girl smiling at him.

FIVE

Janie's New Religion

CONRAD sat in the tower, watching for any sign of the Global Community. He used a flashlight to read a printout of Tsion Ben-Judah's latest teaching. The teaching was so interesting, he had to be careful not to get too absorbed.

Late that night he took a break and closed his eyes for a moment. He ran his hand along the floor and felt a weird bump. A piece of wood stuck up about an inch. He placed his hand on the other side of the plank and pushed. The board gave an inch or two, and Conrad was able to get his fingers underneath.

As he pulled, other boards lifted. Conrad put his flashlight near the hole. Some sort of box fit perfectly inside.

Conrad tried to lift the board, but it

wouldn't budge. The box was decorated with fancy etchings. He shifted his weight to try again, but just then something moved in the woods.

Phoenix growled below. Conrad peered into the darkness and took out his pistol. He quickly ran downstairs and woke Vicki. Vicki let Phoenix loose, and the dog headed for the road, then quickly darted into the woods, barking.

Conrad listened closely. The barking stopped. Footsteps. Had something or someone killed Phoenix? Conrad cocked his pistol and waited.

Three figures moved out of the woods. Conrad lifted the gun and pointed it as he clicked on the flashlight.

"Don't shoot!" Mark said, squinting into the light.

"Mark!" Vicki screamed. "You're back!"

Conrad shone the flashlight on the other two. Melinda and another girl were right behind Mark.

The girl raced toward them. "Vicki!" she shouted.

Vicki stepped back, then hugged the girl and yelled, "Janie!" Vicki looked at Mark. "How did you—?"

"Let's go inside," Mark said, "and we'll tell you all about it."

When Judd awoke the next morning, Lionel was talking with the girl he had seen the night before. Jamal was on the phone speaking in a different language.

"This is Jamal's daughter, Nada," Lionel said.

Judd nodded. Nada smiled and shook his hand.

"Any news on Mr. Stein?" Judd said.

"Haven't been able to understand a word," Lionel said.

Nada spoke with an Arabic accent. "My father still searches for your friend. If anyone can find him, he can."

"How did you become believers?" Judd said.

"My mother was first," Nada said. "When people disappeared around the world, she began reading the theories. Then, when the rabbi spoke on television, she was convinced that Jesus had returned for his true followers."

"Did you know much about Christianity before that?" Lionel said.

Nada shook her head. "We had read the Old Testament that spoke of Abraham. But to us, Christians were unbelievers. When my mother predicted a great earthquake would strike and it happened, my father finally read the rabbi's Web page and received the mark of the believer."

Jamal hung up the phone and quickly dialed another number.

"Who is he calling now?" Lionel said.

Nada listened. "It is a funeral home."

Vicki talked with Janie while Conrad and Mark worked to get Melinda's cuffs off. Melinda seemed happy to be back, but cautious. Vicki hoped to talk with her later. Mark's return was a miracle to Vicki. She was dying to talk with him but knew that would best be done in private.

Vicki looked closely at Janie's forehead. Mark had brought someone who wasn't a believer. She would have to ask him why, but first she wanted to hear Janie's story.

"The last I heard from you," Vicki said, "you'd been taken downstate."

Janie nodded. "I know I gave you and your adoptive dad a hard time after you took me in. I'm really sorry. Where is Bruce?"

Vicki sighed and told Janie that Bruce had died just as the bombs started falling during World War III. "He may have died from a virus he caught overseas, or it could have been the bombing."

"No matter how it happened," Janie said, "he's dead. I'm sorry."

"What happened after you left Chicago?"

Janie said the Global Community had treated her harshly at the first facility, then moved her to one with less security. There she came in contact with the nurse who had helped Vicki take Ryan's body from the makeshift hospital.

"They had her on some kind of charge," Janie said. "We talked a lot about you and religion."

"Religion?" Vicki said.

"Enigma Babylon is what they taught us, and it really turned me around."

Vicki frowned.

"I don't know how I'd have gotten through it without my faith guide," Janie said.

"Your what?"

"We had our own faith guide at the reeducation facility," Janie said. "He taught us that God's within us and we have the power to do anything we want to do."

"What did he say about the Bible?" Vicki said.

Janie shrugged. "We didn't talk about it that much. I guess there are some good stories in there, and some nice teachings, but you really have to follow your own heart if you want to be happy."

Vicki decided not to go further into the Enigma Babylon teaching, but Janie drew close. "That's one reason I wanted to find you. I know you and that Bruce guy, God rest him, follow the Bible. Our faith guide told us how the thing about Adam and Eve, the Flood with Noah, all that stuff's just a myth."

Vicki bit her lip. "What about the prophecies?"

Janie squinted. "What's that?"

"The predictions in the Bible that there would be a worldwide earthquake. The meteors. Wormwood. All that's in the Bible."

"Like I said, we didn't talk much about it," Janie said. "We just learned that God is an idea that lives inside all of us."

"What about heaven and hell?" Vicki said.

"We get what we deserve right here," Janie said. "Heaven's in your head. Besides, why would a God who's supposed to care about us cause all these bad things?"

"Because he wants to get your attention," Vicki said.

"Well, I let my god guide me, and he got me out of that prison."

Vicki got Janie a hot drink and asked Mark to step into the next room. Mark explained what had happened with his aunt and finding Melinda. "I couldn't tell whether Janie was a true believer, but when she mentioned she was trying to find you, I couldn't let her fall into the GC's hands."

Vicki nodded.

"I did a lot of thinking while I was away," Mark said. "I want to stay if you'll let me."

Vicki smiled. "I'm glad you're back."

Judd shuddered when he heard Jamal was talking to someone at a funeral home. When Jamal hung up Judd said, "Is he dead?"

"I must hurry," he said. "One of you goes with me; the other stays here."

"But if he's dead—," Lionel said.

"I cannot discuss it further," Jamal said. He pointed at Lionel. "You come with me."

Judd protested, but Nada put a hand on his arm and shook her head. "You will be here in case there is trouble."

As Jamal put on a hat he said, "Yitzhak is still being questioned. We must pray for him."

When Lionel and Jamal left, Judd and Nada prayed for Yitzhak and the other members of the local committee. Judd then logged on to the Internet to see the latest teaching by Dr. Ben-Judah. Nada noticed an

E-mail that looked like it had come directly from the rabbi.

The E-mail was directed to those on the Tribulation Force. "We have another martyr from our midst," the rabbi wrote. "Ken Ritz was a pilot who helped Buck Williams locate Chloe. He came to faith in Jesus Christ after talking with Buck.

"Ken flew the helicopter that rescued Buck, Chloe, and myself from the Rosenzweig estate in Israel. He was not an American terrorist. He was a hero. While Rayford Steele waited for us at Jerusalem Airport, Ken expertly flew us to the plane. He was shot to death by a Global Community peacekeeper. We will miss him greatly."

Tsion went on to describe some of the ideas Ken Ritz had about feeding believers who would need to go underground after the Global Community required a mark to buy and sell.

"That's exactly what Z is talking about," Judd said. "I hope they get together."

"Z?" Nada said.

Judd explained what he and the Young Trib Force had been through. Nada listened carefully and wiped away a tear when she heard about Bruce, Ryan, Chaya, and John.

Judd hung his head. "And now, Mr. Stein's gone."

Lionel rode in the backseat of Jamal's small car. They wound through the Jerusalem streets that seemed deserted compared to the time of the Meeting of the Witnesses. Lionel wanted to ask questions, but each time Jamal would hold up a hand. "Very dangerous. Must concentrate."

They parked in the back of the funeral home. A hearse was parked with its back door open. Jamal knocked twice at the building, waited, then knocked a third time. A face appeared at the window.

A tall, thin man pointed toward Lionel. The man had circles under his eyes, and his wispy hair was combed over his forehead. "Who is he?"

Jamal explained that Lionel was a friend of Mr. Stein. The man showed them to a nearby room with a wooden coffin.

"You spared no expense," Jamal said.

"This will be lighter for you," the man said as he helped them carry the coffin to the waiting hearse.

"How much for the . . . burial?" Jamal said.

"Get the hearse back this afternoon and we'll call it even," the man said.

Lionel jumped in the back with the coffin.

Jamal shook hands with the man and climbed in behind the wheel.

"What about your car?" Lionel said.

"I will pick it up when I return the hearse," Jamal said.

Lionel looked at the coffin. "I appreciate you doing this, but what are we going to do with the body?"

Jamal ignored Lionel's question and said, "Open the lid and see what kind of shape he is in."

"What?" Lionel could see Jamal's eyes in the rearview mirror.

"They said he was badly beaten at the station," Jamal said. "Open it and tell me how he looks."

Vicki wanted to speak with Melinda about why she had left the kids, but Janie kept talking about Enigma Babylon One World Faith. She didn't seem to think of anyone but herself. When Conrad and Mark cut through the handcuffs, Melinda went to her room to sleep.

"I broke out two days ago," Janie continued. "I slept in a barn the first night and then I found your friends. Lucky break, huh?"

"Yeah," Vicki said. "I'm going to set up

your room, but we have to get some things straight first."

"Shoot," Janie said.

"The stuff that got you into trouble when—"

"The drugs?" Janie said. "I'm clean; you don't have to worry about that."

"Good," Vicki said. "Everybody pitches in with the work here. We take turns with chores and cleaning."

"Yeah, I can handle that," Janie said.

"And we're starting a school in the next few days. We'd like you to try it out as part of our first group of students."

"School for what?" Janie said.

"It'll mostly be studying the Bible. We have material we think will help you. We'll all be studying it."

Janie scowled. "I already have my religion. Don't know what good the Bible will do me."

"Let's give it a week and see what happens," Vicki said.

Lionel took a deep breath. He had seen dead bodies before, but it was different looking at someone he knew and loved.

"Can't it wait till we get . . . to wherever we're going?" Lionel said.

"Open it," Jamal said.

Lionel slowly opened the coffin. Mr. Stein lay peacefully, his eyes closed, his hands folded together. Lionel thought the funeral director had done a good job making him look as lifelike as possible. Mr. Stein had bruises around his eyes and a gash in his lower lip. The funeral director had even put a hint of a smile on the man's face.

"How does he look?" Jamal said.

Lionel shook his head. "I hate to think of what they did to him."

"If you could say one thing to your friend that you didn't get to say, what would it be?" Jamal said.

Lionel closed his eyes and took a deep breath. "I guess I never told him how much I appreciated him. He hadn't been a believer that long, but he motivated all of us to study harder. I'm gonna miss him."

When Lionel opened his eyes, Mr. Stein was sitting up in the coffin, his face inches away.

"And I would say the same to you," Mr. Stein chuckled.

SIX

Mr. Stein's Story

JUDD couldn't believe it when Mr. Stein walked through the door of the apartment. Mr. Stein hugged him, then moved to Nada. "I have heard from Yitzhak what women of faith you and your mother are."

"Yitzhak talks too much," Nada said, blushing.

All Lionel could do was shake his head. "I thought he was dead."

The witnesses who had remained in Jamal's apartment eagerly greeted Mr. Stein. Some spoke in other languages, but Judd could tell they were thanking God their prayers had been answered. As they sat down at the evening meal, Mr. Stein explained what had happened. Nada and Jamal interpreted for the others.

"When the meeting ended that final night,

I accompanied Yitzhak behind the stage to greet Dr. Ben-Judah," Mr. Stein said. "We all thought it might be our last time to express our gratitude to him. The rabbi seemed agitated, like something was wrong. I overheard him talking to Mr. Williams. He said, 'I have a terrible feeling I can only assume is from the Lord.' He wanted to leave quickly, but Mr. Williams could not find his wife and Dr. Rosenzweig. We all looked for them.

"Buck ran away, then a few moments later rushed at Tsion. They hit the ground just as gunfire erupted."

Judd broke in and told them what had happened with the Global Community guard. The witnesses all praised God when Judd told them the guard had become a believer. Mr. Stein picked it up from there.

"GC guards ran to the stage as the gunfire began," Mr. Stein continued. "Buck grabbed Dr. Ben-Judah and ran for their car. The local committee provided a few obstacles."

"What do you mean?" Lionel said.

"We stood in front of the exits and blocked the guards," Mr. Stein said. "We thought it was the least we could do for Tsion."

Witnesses laughed. "What happened then?" Lionel said.

"They shot their guns in the air to frighten

us, but we were not about to allow them to shoot at our leader."

"Did that stop them?" Judd said.

Mr. Stein smiled. "We gave the rabbi and the others a few extra moments to get away. The guards finally got through us, but not before Tsion and the others escaped."

"Is that when you were arrested?" Judd said.

Mr. Stein nodded. "I have never been treated so roughly in my life. They held their guns to our heads and led us to a GC van parked near the entrance to the stadium. We sang praises to God and encouraged each other with verses we had memorized.

"I said to Yitzhak, if Paul and Silas can pray all night in prison, so can we."

The witnesses seated around him sent up another cheer.

"Daniel stood in the van as it careened around the streets. He shouted, 'We are pressed on every side by troubles, but we are not crushed and broken. We are perplexed, but we don't give up and quit.' Another said, 'We are hunted down, but God never abandons us. We get knocked down, but we get up again and keep going.' And Yitzhak finished the verse, saying, 'Through suffering, these bodies of ours constantly share in the death of Jesus so that the life of Jesus may also be seen in our bodies.'

"When we stood before the Global Community officers, each of us was asked why we were a follower of Dr. Ben-Judah. I learned later that each of us answered with the apostle Paul's words, 'I believe in God, and so I speak!'"

The witnesses around the room lifted their hands and praised God. Some whispered; others shouted. Mr. Stein held up a hand.

"I had no idea the enemy would inflict so much punishment on us. They knocked us down and made us suffer greatly. They beat me again and again, asking me where they could find the rabbi and the others. But I do not know, so how could I tell them?"

Mr. Stein smiled, then grew serious. "At one point yesterday, I believe they planned to kill me. They knew I was the only American in the group and believed I had to know more than I had told them, which was nothing. They had treated me so badly they knew there was nothing they could do to make me give them information about my friends.

"So I waited and prayed. Yitzhak was in the next cell. We prayed together for courage and strength. We were both so exhausted, so spent from the mistreatment.

"And then, at our lowest point, we heard a

noise. Faint, down the hallway. I went to the front, pressed my ear between the iron bars, and heard a sound I will take with me to the Glorious Appearing of our Great God."

Judd leaned closer. Mr. Stein stopped, overcome with emotion. "What was it?" Judd said.

Mr. Stein looked up, tears in his eyes. "Singing," he whispered. "I heard a dear brother—I cannot tell you who he was—but he began the little song I have never heard, but I will never forget."

Mr. Stein softly sang the words Judd knew were from the Doxology. They had sung it at his church at least once a month when he was a kid, and it had meant nothing to him then. Now the words sent a chill throughout his body.

"Praise God from whom all blessings flow. Praise him, all creatures here below. Praise him above, ye heavenly host. Praise Father, Son, and Holy Ghost. Amen."

Witnesses wept as they quietly sang along with Mr. Stein. "Forgive my voice," he said. "The only place my wife would let me sing was in the shower."

Everyone laughed.

"But I am sure that sound brought joy to

our heavenly Father. We were praising him in the midst of our trouble.

"We sang the song over and over, until I learned all the words. Then, Yitzhak recited something from the Psalms. I do not recall the entire verse, but it talked about committing your way to the Lord. It was very powerful."

A barrel-chested man stood meekly in the corner. His voice was strong and clear as he recited from Psalm 37. "'Commit everything you do to the Lord. Trust him, and he will help you. He will make your innocence as clear as the dawn, and the justice of your cause will shine like the noonday sun. Be still in the presence of the Lord, and wait patiently for him to act. Don't worry about evil people who prosper or fret about their wicked schemes.'"

"That's it!" Mr. Stein said. "And that is exactly what we did. In the midst of suffering and possible death, our hearts were knit together. The fear I had was gone. I knew if I lived, I would give glory to God. If I died, I would be with my wife and daughter, and with my Lord. Wherever I was, I would give glory to God."

Mr. Stein wiped his eyes and sat. His shoulders shook with emotion. Finally, he spoke. "I fell into a deep sleep. It had nothing to do with the mistreatment by the guards. I simply drifted off and slept like a little child.

"When I awoke, I discovered they had taken me into a sort of doctor's office. There were beds around the room and a huge, metal refrigerator with compartments for bodies."

"The morgue!" Lionel said.

"Exactly," Mr. Stein said. "I had gone into such a deep sleep that somehow they believed I was dead."

"Didn't they check your pulse?" Judd said.

"I have no doubt that they did," Mr. Stein said, "but I do not know why they could not feel it. Either God blinded their eyes or he made it so faint that they could not detect it. How he did it, I do not know, but that the tall man did it I am sure.

"A tall man and his assistant wheeled me to a hearse. Once I almost sneezed, but I was able to control it. I kept my eyes closed until we reached the funeral home. That is when I opened my eyes and saw that the tall man had the mark of the believer on his forehead. When he came close, I reached out and grabbed his arm.

"I raised up on the bed and said, 'The Lord be with you, my brother!' and the man nearly fainted dead away."

Witnesses around the room laughed and shouted with joy.

"And here I am," Mr. Stein said, "a testimony to the grace of God, a picture of the goodness and provision of God. May he alone be praised."

With that, the people around the room clapped and commended Mr. Stein on his faith. Behind Judd, a small voice began the strain again. Judd turned and saw Nada, singing through tears, "Praise God from whom all blessings flow...."

Vicki and Mark spoke briefly with Melinda the next morning. Melinda apologized for putting the group in danger and thanked Mark again. "If he hadn't helped me, I wouldn't be here right now."

"And if I hadn't gone to see about my aunt," Mark said, "I wouldn't have had any reason to be there."

"God works everything for good," Vicki said, "even disagreements." Vicki told Melinda about the school.

Melinda seemed hesitant but gave her word that she would attend classes at least the first week. "I'm not sure I buy into everything you guys believe," Melinda said, "but

I'm pretty sure you're right about the Global Community."

Vicki and Conrad met with Mark to discuss the mysterious E-mail messages that had been coming in for Mark. The same message asking for him to respond immediately had appeared again, and it concerned Conrad.

"I think the safest thing we could do is delete the thing and not respond," Conrad said.

Mark studied the message. "It's definitely from a GC post. How would they get our E-mail address, and why would they want to write me?"

"Have you answered any of Tsion's E-mails?" Conrad said. "They could have gotten the address from that."

"Some, but not nearly as many as Judd," Mark said. "It just doesn't make sense."

"Unless it's from somebody who knew John," Vicki said.

Mark nodded. "That's a possibility, but how do we know they're friendly? Maybe whoever wrote met John and he ticked them off."

"What would it hurt to try?" Vicki said. "They can't trace our location from the E-mail, right?"

Mark nodded and read the message again. "Vicki's right. We ought to try." Mark wrote a quick reply that read: "I'm not sure I can trust you. Explain your intentions."

Vicki asked, "What now?"

Mark sat back. "Wait to see what he says."

Judd stayed with Mr. Stein and listened to more witnesses share their stories. Some seemed as amazing as Mr. Stein's. One man described how he had walked a hundred miles, then traveled by camel, by boat, and finally by plane to get to the Meeting of the Witnesses. His food and water ran out the second day of his journey, but God had provided. At one point he thought he would pass out from thirst, but there came a downpour, and the man caught rainwater in his hat. When he had enough to drink, the rain stopped.

"Our God is awesome," the man said.

Nada touched Judd's shoulder. "You have a phone call from Samuel."

Samuel was still out of breath when Judd picked up the phone. "I'm very sorry about your friend, Mr. Stein," Samuel said. "He is dead."

Judd asked for more information, not letting Samuel know the truth about Mr. Stein. He didn't want Samuel to know more than he had to.

"My father is still very upset. He wants to catch Ben-Judah and the others who have made the GC look bad. They think you might be able to lead them there."

"We have no idea where the rabbi is hiding," Judd said.

"I believe you," Samuel said, "but you must be very careful. They have increased security at all the airports in the country. They suspect you will try to leave soon. And my father says they have a plan to catch you."

"Thanks for the info," Judd said. "You'd better be careful yourself."

"I do not think he suspects anything," Samuel said.

"Have you thought about what we talked about?" Judd said.

Samuel sounded agitated. "I think I see my father's car!"

"Go!" Judd shouted. "And call me back when you get the chance."

Judd hung up. Mr. Stein took him and Lionel aside. "I have been given a wonderful opportunity. I did not want to talk about it in front of the others."

"What kind of opportunity?" Judd said.

"Yitzhak and the others on the local committee want me to stay and learn from them. They have agreed to teach me about the Scriptures. It is exactly what I've been looking for."

Judd was excited for him but couldn't help wondering how he and Lionel would get home then.

"I know you want to return to your friends," Mr. Stein said. "I will arrange a commercial flight for you both."

Judd told them what Samuel had said about the airports.

"That will make it more difficult," Mr. Stein said.

"Do you still have your money?" Lionel said.

"I sensed there might be a problem, so I hid it at the university."

"So all we have to do is get it and find a way back," Judd said.

Mr. Stein nodded. "What about Taylor Graham's friend in Tel Aviv?"

"Hasina!" Lionel said. "She'd help us!"

Mr. Stein looked at the ceiling and wiped away a tear. "Call her first thing in the morning. Perhaps she will come through."

"What's wrong?" Judd said.

"Throughout this ordeal I thought of Chaya," Mr. Stein said. "She would have loved to see me at the Meeting of the Witnesses and hear Tsion speak."

"I bet she was watching," Lionel said.

Mr. Stein smiled. "It's clear we must retrieve the money, but we have a problem. Neither you nor I should be seen in public."

"I will go," Nada said.

Judd turned. He didn't know she had been listening.

"I'm the same age as many of the students," Nada said, "and I blend in much better than you Americans."

"We'll talk about this in the morning," Mr. Stein said. He went to his room.

"I can do it," Nada said.

Judd nodded. "We'll run it past your dad in the morning. Maybe he has a contact who can get us in."

Nada said good night and returned to her family's apartment. Judd grabbed Lionel's arm. "I can't wait till tomorrow to call Hasina. Let's try her now!"

Judd found her card and dialed the number. It rang several times before Hasina's answering machine picked up. Judd left a message about needing a flight home, but he thought it too dangerous to leave Jamal's number. He told Hasina he would call the next morning at 9 A.M. Judd wondered if she would be able to help them. She was their best chance to make it back to the States.

SEVEN

Lionel's Search

VICKI checked E-mail late that night in Illinois. She was relieved to see a message from Judd. He briefly explained what had happened at Teddy Kollek Stadium and how Mr. Stein had escaped a Global Community prison.

"We're trying to get back as fast as we can, but there may be problems," Judd wrote. "I'll write again and tell when you can expect us. Lionel sends his best and so do I. Hope things have worked out with Melinda. Judd."

Vicki frowned. When Judd was gone from the group she felt an emptiness that wouldn't go away. When he was there, he and Vicki fought. She still had feelings for him, still missed him, but she had no idea what to do with those feelings.

She pushed the thoughts from her mind and scanned the other messages. She sat up straight when she saw another E-mail to Mark. It was from the same person who had written earlier from the GC. She called out to Mark.

Mark came quickly. Vicki read over Mark's shoulder as he opened the message.

> Dear Mark,
>
> My intentions are pure. I'm at a GC outpost in South Carolina, recovering from injuries I received on the *Peacekeeper 1*. Your cousin, John Preston, saved my life.
>
> I want to meet with you. I'd like to tell you what happened, since the GC has kept the story quiet. Can you come here? If not, I can come to you as soon as I'm released from the hospital.
>
> Please write and let me know. You can trust me.
>
> Sincerely,
> Carl Meninger

Mark scratched his chin. He opened a computer filing cabinet filled with other E-mails.

"What are you doing?" Vicki said.

"That name sounds familiar," Mark said. He did a search of the name *Meninger* and came up with nothing. Then he typed in the name *Carl*. A single E-mail appeared on the screen. It was John's last message.

"This is it," Mark said.

At the end of the message John had written, "Someday I hope you meet Carl. He can tell you what happened here. No time now. Just enough to say I love you all. Keep fighting the good fight. We'll be cheering you on. Never give up. John."

"You think it's the same Carl?" Vicki said.

"Has to be," Mark said. "John says he hopes we get to meet him. That's enough for me."

"What if it's a GC trick?"

Mark raised his eyebrows. "Now who's the one being too cautious?"

Vicki smiled.

Mark answered the E-mail, saying that he would love to meet Carl, but he could not get to South Carolina any time soon. Mark suggested that Carl write about his experience with John or set up a phone call.

"I wonder how he survived the meteor?" Vicki said.

When Judd awoke the next morning, he heard Mr. Stein and Nada talking in the next room. He called Hasina again but hung up when he reached her answering machine. By the time Judd joined them, Nada was gone.

Judd could tell that Mr. Stein was upset, and in the morning light he saw more clearly the bruises about the man's head. It was a miracle he had gotten out of the GC questioning alive.

Before Mr. Stein could explain what they had talked about, Jamal came in the room. He spoke through clenched teeth as he looked at Mr. Stein.

"Stay away from my daughter, and stop filling her head with these crazy ideas!"

"Believe me," Mr. Stein said, "I told her I couldn't put her life in danger—"

Jamal looked at Judd. "You put her up to this!"

"Is this about Mr. Stein's money?" Judd said.

"You care more about your own lives than you do hers," Jamal said.

Judd started to explain that Nada had volunteered to get the money, but Mr. Stein put up a hand. "Trust me; we will speak no more of this to her."

Jamal stared at them. "I will not lose another child." He slammed the door as he left.

"What was that about?" Judd said.

Lionel walked in. Mr. Stein offered him some breakfast. "Did Nada tell you how she became a believer?"

Judd nodded. "She said her mother believed first."

"Did she say anything about her brother?"

Judd was puzzled. "I didn't even know she had a brother. Jamal never said anything about him."

"Yitzhak told me their story while we were detained," Mr. Stein said. "Just as the rest of the family believed that Jesus is the Savior, Jamal's son, Kasim, believed that Nicolae Carpathia was the way to peace and happiness. They had many arguments about it."

"Just like in your family," Lionel said.

Mr. Stein nodded. "Except I finally agreed with my daughter. Kasim was killed before he came to the truth."

"What happened?" Judd said.

Mr. Stein sat back and folded his hands. "Yitzhak said Nada was very bold with her brother. Kasim was three years older, but she would not back away from telling him the truth.

"Kasim was so committed to Carpathia that he volunteered to become a GC guard. Even while he was training, Nada would come into the Global Community compound and speak with Kasim openly about Christ."

"That girl knows no fear," Lionel said.

"Maybe she just loved her brother," Judd said. "Was he accepted into the GC?"

"He was assigned to security in New Babylon," Mr. Stein said, "to the main building where Nicolae Carpathia kept his office."

"The earthquake!" Judd said.

"Exactly," Mr. Stein said. "He was on the ground floor when the quake hit. Jamal and his wife received a letter of sorrow and thanks from the potentate just after the mass funeral. They never found Kasim's body."

"I'm sure Nick's letter meant a lot to them," Judd said sarcastically.

"You see why I did not challenge Jamal," Mr. Stein said. "He has been through much pain. I can understand him wanting to protect his only living child."

"We'll have to get the money ourselves," Judd said.

"How are we going to get inside the gymnasium?" Lionel said.

Mr. Stein pulled out a key. "Yitzhak gave me this. It is to the back entrance. Perhaps one of us should go, rather than all three."

They drew straws. Lionel's was the shortest. "Looks like I'm headed back to the university," he said.

In the excitement of Mark's return with Melinda and Janie, Conrad hadn't forgotten what he had seen in the tower. The next day he climbed to the top and inspected the board again. He put a foot on one end and tried to pry it loose, but when he did, he noticed something he hadn't seen the night before. Four boards were attached together.

Conrad inspected the others and found a tiny hook barely visible under the middle boards. He retrieved a screwdriver and tripped the hook. The boards lifted easily.

Conrad gasped when he saw the ancient box in the daylight. It was two feet square with fancy carvings on top. The box was made of thick metal, and a huge lock hung on the front.

Conrad knelt and strained to lift the box. It was almost more than he could carry. He struggled down the stairs into the meeting room and dropped it on the floor. It fell with such a crash that the kids came running from all over the house.

Vicki ran a hand over the ornate etchings on top. "You think this is what Z was talking about?"

Conrad shrugged. "When he talked about a safe, I thought it would be five feet tall. But this is sure old."

Mark looked closely. "This lock's going to take some time to open."

Janie stepped forward. "Are we gonna split what's inside evenly?" When Vicki didn't answer, Janie said, "I mean, if there's anything valuable inside. I just want to be fair."

"This isn't our house to begin with," Vicki said. "If there's anything of value inside, Z would need to make that call."

"Right," Janie said. "I didn't know this wasn't your house. Sorry."

Shelly, who had wandered off, called for the others from the next room. "Judd just sent a message. He asked us to pray for Lionel. He's evidently doing something pretty dangerous."

Lionel felt queasy about going to the university but glad that Jamal had agreed to drive him in his small car. In the afternoon, Lionel and Judd helped Jamal move large boxes up the freight elevator and into the hideout. Jamal spoke very little, clearly still upset about what he thought they had asked Nada to do.

"What are these for?" Judd said.

"You will see" was all Jamal would say.

Lionel put on a long robe and turban Nada had found. "One of the witnesses left it behind," she said. The outfit dragged the floor, and Lionel felt goofy.

"I don't care if it makes me look less Amer-

ican," Lionel said "If they catch me, they'll
call the GC."

Lionel left the disguise and climbed into
the tiny backseat of Jamal's car. He lay on the
seat as Jamal wound through the Old City.
Several times Jamal warned Lionel to keep
down as he spotted Global Community
squad cars.

Finally, they came near the university. Lionel sat up. Teddy Kollek Stadium was deserted.
Yellow tape circled many of the university
buildings where the witnesses had stayed.

Jamal pulled close to the gymnasium and
handed Lionel his cell phone. "This is in case
you have trouble finding what you're looking
for," Jamal said. "I'll wait on the other side of
the street until you give the signal."

Lionel felt inside his pocket for the flashlight. He hoped there would be no cameras
or alarms in the building.

Judd and Mr. Stein prayed for Lionel as they
waited for him to return. Nada handed Judd
the phone. It was Samuel again.

"Did your father catch you outside last
night?" Judd said.

"No," Samuel said, "but I don't have time
to talk. I called to warn you."

"About what?" Judd said.

"The GC found something at the university where Mr. Stein was staying," Samuel said. "They have guards there in case someone shows up!"

"Thanks," Judd said. He hung up without saying good-bye and ran for Nada. "What's your dad's cell phone number?"

Lionel let his eyes adjust to the darkness and tried the key. Wrong door. He walked to the end of the building and tried again. This time the lock clicked, and he walked inside.

The cots had been removed from the gym floor. Lionel tiptoed across the hardwood floor, but his footsteps still echoed. He scanned the door for anything suspicious.

Lionel pulled out the map Mr. Stein had drawn and found the hallway leading to a small office. He looked along the wall for the fire extinguisher but couldn't find it.

He pulled out the cell phone and dialed Jamal's house. The line was busy.

Something moved in the gym. Footsteps. Voices. Lionel turned off his flashlight and darted into an open doorway. He was in the men's room. He backed against a wall and listened, his heart pounding furiously.

"What did they say?" one man said.

"Get out your gun," the other man said. "Campus police said somebody was just at the back of the gym."

Lionel dialed Jamal's number again. Judd answered.

"Let me talk with Mr. Stein, quick!" Lionel whispered.

"No!" Judd said. "Get out of there! The GC has guards waiting for you."

The back door opened.

"I might as well try," Lionel whispered. "Let me talk with Mr. Stein!"

"Please, Lionel," Mr. Stein said, "get out now."

"Just tell me again," Lionel said. "I can't find the fire extinguish—"

"Do you see the office?"

"Yeah, I'm in the men's room across the hall."

"You are at the wrong end," Mr. Stein said. "Go the other direction down the hall."

"Got it," Lionel whispered. He hurried from the bathroom and down the hall, being careful not to make noise. He found the fire extinguisher behind a glass door.

The gym door closed. The guards were coming. Lionel heard Mr. Stein plead with him to get out. Lionel opened the door to the fire extinguisher slowly. Someone honked their horn. *Jamal,* Lionel thought. The guards took the bait and ran for the back door.

Lionel pulled the fire extinguisher out of the wall and felt behind it. Nothing. He switched on the flashlight and saw a small bag at the bottom. He picked it up and looked inside.

"The money's not here," Lionel said.

Suddenly an alarm sounded.

EIGHT

Hasina's News

LIONEL knew the alarm was somehow attached to the empty bag. He dropped the fire extinguisher and ran into the gym. The guards rushed inside. Lionel had a head start on them, but not much.

He ran into a long hallway. He looked right, then left. At the left end was an Exit sign. He sprinted toward it, then realized as he got closer that the sign pointed down another hallway.

"There he goes," a guard yelled behind him.

Lionel didn't slow down. He rounded the corner and bounced off a row of lockers. Through light, then shadows, he careened down the hall. A red sign was posted over the door at the end of the hallway: ALARM WILL SOUND. PLEASE USE OTHER EXIT. He hit the red lever full force, and another alarm screamed

over his head. He flung the door open and
raced into the cool air.

He had hoped Jamal would be waiting, but
the man was nowhere in sight. Lionel cursed,
then realized what he had said and shook his
head.

He sprinted to the right and into the darkness beside the building. The door opened
behind him, and both guards raced out. One
fired his gun, but Lionel kept running.

"Go that way! I'll follow him," a guard said.

Lionel rounded the corner and was nearly
hit by Jamal's car, its lights off. "Get in
quickly!" Jamal yelled.

Lionel opened the back door and yelled,
"Go!" He jumped inside, hitting his head
against the other door as Jamal floored the gas
pedal of the tiny car. As Jamal rounded the
corner, he turned on his lights and blinded
the guard running toward them. The guard
threw a hand over his eyes and shot wildly at
the small car, the bullet pinging off the hood.

"Stay down!" Jamal shouted.

Jamal zigged and zagged until they were
out of the parking lot and into the street. The
GC guards followed, but they were no match
for Jamal's knowledge of the city. He took
alleys and backstreets until he arrived safely
in the parking garage of the apartment building.

Judd and Mr. Stein hugged Lionel when he returned. Lionel filled them in on what had happened.

"They must have found your money when they searched the building," Judd said. "What do we do now?"

"Maybe Hasina will take an IOU," Lionel said.

Mr. Stein said, "God will provide."

Judd tried Hasina's number again, and his eyes widened. "It's busy!"

"Keep trying," Lionel said.

Before dinner, Vicki had a chance to talk more with Melinda. The girl seemed less angry and a little more open since she had returned.

"I just couldn't stay here," Melinda said. "Listening to all those prophecies, all the bad stuff to come, knowing that it might be true. It just overwhelmed me."

"How do you feel now?" Vicki said.

"Afraid I'll be the one who leads the GC here."

"We have people watching around the clock," Vicki said. "And we always have a way to escape if we have to."

Melinda pulled her hair from her face. "I

want to go to your classes and all that, but I'm still not sure if I can believe the way you guys do."

"You mean you're not sure if what we're saying is true?"

Melinda shook her head. "I'm pretty convinced you're on the right track. I'm just not sure I can study the Bible. Still feels a little weird to me."

"If you'll ask God into your heart, it won't feel weird. I remember when I did it. It was a couple of years ago. I'd never even thought of what would happen to me after I died. Reading the Bible was for losers. Then I realized it was true. Practical. What I read in the Bible every day helps me. Every day is a new chance to really live."

Mark walked into the room holding a few sheets of paper. He had a blank stare on his face.

"What's wrong with you?" Melinda said.

"I can't believe we missed it," Mark said.

"Missed what?" Vicki said.

"Tsion's message from the Meeting of the Witnesses. It's all right here, and we missed it."

Vicki took the paper and scanned the message. "I remember hearing this. Tsion said the sun, moon, and stars are going to be affected by the next judgment."

"Don't you see what that means?" Mark said.

"We'll have a third less light," Vicki said, "but that's what the generator's for."

"You don't understand," Mark said. "A third less solar energy means disaster. The whole planet's going into the deep freeze."

"We happen to be out in the middle of the woods," Melinda said. "If what's been predicted actually happens, we can just cut down some trees and throw another log on the fire."

Mark shook his head. "You still don't get it. I've worked it out on the computer. The temperature's not going down by a third. You cut direct sunlight like this and we're all in big trouble. People are going to die."

Judd dialed Hasina again and again. Finally, on the tenth try, the phone rang and Hasina picked up, out of breath. "Taylor, I'm not ready!" Hasina yelled.

"It's Judd Thompson! What's wrong?"

"Judd, the GC are chasing Taylor. He tried to take out another installation. He's on his way here. I have to get his plane ready."

Hasina took the cordless phone with her as she walked through the steps to start the plane.

"I know this is not the time to ask," Judd said, "but Lionel and I need a ride out of Israel. Our money is gone. The GC took it. Is there a chance—"

"Taylor wants me to go with him," Hasina said. "He believes the GC know about our operation. Perhaps we'll get set up in another city and we can fly you from there."

Judd heard a clanking sound and figured Hasina was opening the hangar door. Seconds later, the plane's engine fired.

"Where do you think you'll go?" Judd said.

"Spain, perhaps," Hasina said. "Taylor has a friend there who has said he will help us." She gasped.

"What is it?" Judd said.

"I see Taylor's car! The GC are right behind him."

"Get out on the runway!" Judd shouted.

"I can't," Hasina said. "They already have it blocked."

"Is there a place you can hide?"

"Oh no," Hasina said, "they have him trapped."

Judd closed his eyes and listened. He could hear sirens blaring in the background. He thought of Taylor's escape from the earthquake. Judd had thought Taylor was dead when the raging waters had taken him over the edge of a chasm, but Taylor had survived. Was there any way he could survive this?

"Look," Judd said, "Taylor will never let them take him alive. He'll put up a fight. That should give you time to hide!"

A gun went off. Then another. Then a *pop-pop-pop* of automatic fire.

"It's no use," Hasina said, her voice full of despair. "They have him."

"What do you mean?"

"They shot him as he sat in the car, and they're coming this way."

"Hasina, get out of there!" Judd shouted. He turned to Lionel and Mr. Stein. "Pray, and pray hard!"

"I'm putting the phone in my shirt pocket so you can hear what happens," Hasina said. "If we do not make it, good luck."

Judd heard the door to the plane open. The phone was muffled for a moment as Hasina put the phone away. She breathed heavily as she ran. Someone shouted, "There she is!" A few shots rang out.

A door opened and closed. Hasina moved furniture to get to something. Keys jangled.

Judd turned on the speakerphone and turned it all the way up. Mr. Stein and Lionel leaned close. They heard Hasina open a door with the keys. It sounded like she was loading a weapon of some sort.

Then someone banged on the door. Something fell to the floor, and Hasina cursed.

"Open it now!" someone shouted.

"Shoot them!" Taylor Graham said from the other side.

Hasina was breathing hard and scrambling on the floor to pick up what had fallen. Two huge gunshots exploded, and the door banged open.

"Drop it now!" a voice boomed.

"Shoot them!" Taylor screamed, his voice louder now that the door was open.

"I said shut up!" a man yelled, and Judd heard a whack and a crunch of bone.

"Taylor!" Hasina shouted.

"Put the gun down," another man said.

Something clattered to the floor.

"Good, now step away from the desk, your hands in the air."

Hasina was breathing heavily now. She spoke with her teeth clenched. "Do you know what this is?" she said. "We rigged this just in case something like this happened."

"Put it down!"

"I push this button, and the whole place goes up. You shoot me, and I swear I'll take you all with me."

A GC officer clicked his radio. "There's a

bomb. The girl's threatening to blow the whole place up. Everybody out!"

"Leave Taylor and get out of here, and I'll let you live!"

The radio crackled. "Confirm explosive!" someone said.

Hasina barked, "This is hooked to the underground jet fuel. Now unless you want to all go up with us, leave now!"

The GC officer spoke into his walkie-talkie. He ordered everyone to move a safe distance away. Hasina ran to Taylor Graham and spoke his name.

Judd felt almost guilty, listening. These were such private moments, and Hasina had either forgotten that Judd was on the line or didn't care.

"Taylor, I love you."

Taylor's voice was groggy. "I love you, too. Always have. If I'd have married you like I promised, we wouldn't be in this mess. We'd probably have five or six kids by now and be living on a beach somewhere."

Hasina laughed. Taylor sounded close to the phone. "We don't have to worry about what might have been," she said. "We both made our choices."

"Did you really rig the place to explode?" Taylor said.

"I control everything with this," Hasina said. She giggled. "It's my lipstick case."

"Pretty convincing," Taylor said, and then he cried out in pain. "I'm bleeding to death. I think they hit an artery in my leg."

Hasina moved. Judd heard a cloth ripping.

"It's no use," Taylor said. "They're going to figure out you don't have explosives in here."

Judd had a million questions. How had the GC discovered Taylor? Was Judd partly responsible since he told the GC guard about him?

"Try to make it back to the plane," Taylor gasped. "There's a chance you could get around them to the runway."

"You know that's not possible now," Hasina said. "Listen. More GC cars are on their way."

"We could ask for a personal audience with Nicolae Carpathia," Taylor said.

"Other than marrying you, that is the only thing I wanted to do in this life."

"Somebody else will have the privilege," Taylor said. "If that Thompson kid and his friends are right—"

"Judd!" Hasina said. She pulled the phone out of her pocket. "Are you still there?"

Judd picked up the phone on his end. "We're here."

"I guess you've heard we're in a pretty tight spot." She handed the phone to Taylor.

"I wish we could be there to help you," Judd said. "I'm sorry. I feel responsible—"

"I made more than one mistake trying to shoot that guy down," Taylor said. "It's not your fault I'm in this mess."

Mr. Stein asked to talk to them, so Judd flipped on the speakerphone again. "Taylor, you may not have much longer to live. We've told you about Jesus. If you die without him—"

"Save your breath," Taylor said. He passed the phone to Hasina.

"Hasina, I talked with you about Jesus," Judd said. "If you ask him to forgive you—"

"I'm sorry, Judd," Hasina said. "I appreciate your concern and your love, but a last-minute step of faith is not for me."

"The thief on the cross asked for forgiveness and received it," Lionel said.

Something banged in the background. The phone dropped to the floor. Guards were back. "We checked your tanks. They're not wired."

Judd heard a smack. Hasina cried out.

"It's lipstick!" the guard sneered.

"Don't hurt her!" Taylor shouted.

A gun went off.

"Taylor!" Hasina screamed.

"You were part of the plot to kill the potentate," the guard said.

"I would gladly pull the trigger," Hasina said.

The gun fired again. "You will not have the chance," the guard muttered. He clicked his walkie-talkie. "Both suspects are dead. They resisted arrest, and we were forced to kill them."

"Liar," Judd muttered.

Another guard entered. "What should we do with the crime scene, Commander?"

"Burn it."

The guard ran away. Someone picked up the phone. Judd heard breathing on the other end. "Who is there?" the man said.

"You won't get away with this," Judd said. He hung up the phone.

NINE

Fracture in the Family

VICKI looked at Mark's prediction on the computer. Though she was never that good at math, his numbers seemed right. At dinner she announced an all-out effort to store fuel.

"We have enough food to keep us going a few months," Vicki said, "but if Mark is right about what's coming, we need to insulate the problem areas and get more fuel."

"What fuel?" Janie said.

"Firewood," Vicki said, "enough to last a couple months."

Janie sighed. "Thought I was done with grunt labor when I escaped the GC camp."

Vicki ignored her. "Conrad, I need you to coordinate the around-the-clock GC lookout from the tower."

"Already done," Conrad said. "We do three eight-hour shifts. Shelly's up there right now."

"Any luck with the box?" Vicki said.

Conrad shook his head. "I've broken three saw blades on it so far."

"It'll have to take a backseat to this," Vicki said. "As a matter of fact, we'll have to postpone classes, too."

"What happens if his predictions don't come true?" Melinda said. "We're already into spring. Summer's not far away. How's it going to get that cold this time of year?"

"Yeah," Janie said, "we could work our tails off for nothing."

Mark scowled. "Dr. Ben-Judah's been predicting stuff since the GC made their treaty with Israel. He hasn't been wrong yet."

Judd was crushed by the deaths of Taylor and Hasina. He wanted to call the media and tell them the truth about what happened, but he knew the media was controlled by Nicolae Carpathia. A sense of despair set in. Not only had they lost two friends, but they had also lost their best chance of getting home.

Judd went to his room and tried to sleep, but couldn't. He composed an E-mail and sent it to Conrad, then fixed a cup of coffee. His father had been a big-time coffee drinker, but his mother had warned Judd not to start.

In his senior year he had pulled several all-nighters with nothing but sheer willpower and a thermos filled with coffee.

Now, as Judd held the hot cup and thought about his family, it seemed like two different lives. Only a little more than two years had passed since the vanishings. In those two years his life had turned upside down. Nothing was constant. He seemed to always be on the run.

He longed for some kind of stability. He thought of Vicki. Maybe her idea about the school was best. Judd regretted his harsh words and disagreements with her. If he could start over again, things would be different.

A door opened behind him. Nada sat down. "Couldn't sleep?"

Judd shook his head.

"I heard about your friends. I'm very sorry."

"I knew Taylor would go too far sooner or later," Judd said, "but I really hoped Hasina would come to believe in Jesus."

"It is the same way I felt about my brother," Nada said. She tucked her feet under her and leaned back. "I talked with him the night before he died. He was so excited about seeing Leon Fortunato in the hallway."

Judd sighed in disgust. "Leon came to my school once. The guy's a weasel."

"He is worse than that," Nada said. "My father believes he is the false prophet." She waved her hand. "Enough about Fortunato. My brother could not stop talking about the lavish lifestyle the Global Community provided him. He was only a guard, but he said his apartment was like a palace compared to our house."

"It's hard for people to think about heaven when they feel like they have it here," Judd said.

"I think in his heart, he knew the truth. He told me he had seen and heard things that troubled him. The potentate seemed loving and giving to the public, but behind the scenes he could be ruthless."

"So your brother was coming around."

"Not quickly enough. I told him about Dr. Ben-Judah and his teaching. My brother knew all about him. He said he was Public Enemy Number One with the GC."

"Had he read anything Tsion wrote?"

"He saw the news broadcast when Dr. Ben-Judah announced that Jesus was the true Messiah of the Jews," Nada said.

"Mr. Stein said you received a personal letter from the potentate after his death."

Nada went to a cabinet just inside the front door and found a photo album. She turned the pages carefully until she came to

Kasim's picture. "This is us on holiday in Greece when we were kids." Standing beside a huge sand castle, Nada and Kasim smiled at the camera. Jamal and his wife knelt behind them, the Mediterranean Sea in the background.

Judd stared at the photo. He thought of his own family album and photos at their cottage on Lake Michigan or on vacation in Florida.

Nada flipped the pages and couldn't hold back the tears. "When I see my brother, I can only think of what might have been. What God might have done through him."

Judd put an arm around her. He wanted to say something, anything, but he could think of nothing. They spent the rest of the night looking through the album and telling stories of their families.

Vicki showed Conrad Judd's E-mail about Taylor. Conrad pursed his lips. "I knew it would happen if he didn't change, but it's still hard."

Vicki put an arm around him. "If you need to take some time, I understand."

Over the next few days, Vicki supervised the storing of wood near the schoolhouse while Mark, Conrad, and Charlie worked in the forest, gathering firewood. Each evening Mark would fill Vicki in on how much help Charlie had been.

"I know I complained about him coming here at first," Mark said, "but that guy can really handle an ax!"

Vicki's most difficult task was keeping an eye on Janie. She was constantly taking a rest and grumbling about doing so much manual labor. Melinda even commented in private about Janie's poor attitude.

As the temperature rose one day, Vicki went to the kitchen to fix some cool drinks. Vicki found Janie in the main meeting room, her feet on the table, watching a music video on the computer.

"What are you doing?" Vicki said.

Janie whirled, her feet hitting the floor hard. "You almost scared me to death!"

"Why aren't you outside helping?"

"Do you know how hot it is out there?" Janie said. "And we're stacking firewood like our lives depend on it."

"Our lives may very well depend on it," Vicki said.

Janie scoffed. "Even back at the camp, we got to watch videos and stuff. Here, all we do is work."

"You know this computer's not for entertainment," Vicki said, disconnecting from the Web site.

"I'm going to my room," Janie shouted. "I need a day off."

Vicki recalled how difficult Janie had been at Bruce's house. She wouldn't follow the rules there either. Nothing had changed in her life except her move toward the Enigma Babylon Faith. Vicki wondered if she would hang on to that belief after the next judgment hit.

Lionel noticed Judd and Nada were spending more time together. They talked till late at night. Many afternoons they exercised together on the rooftop. Lionel asked Mr. Stein if he should say something to Judd.

"What would you say?" Mr. Stein said. "These things happen between males and females."

"I understand that," Lionel said, "but if he gets too involved here, he may not want to go back to the States."

"Perhaps that is what God wants," Mr. Stein said. "None of us knows what will happen in the future."

Jamal asked Mr. Stein, Judd, and Lionel to remain with them until they heard from Yitzhak. "As long as you're here, you should

be safe," Jamal said. Lionel knew he and
Judd would be on their own if Yitzhak were
released.

Jamal kept quiet about the mountain of
boxes Judd and Lionel had carried to the
apartment. Things were getting tight in many
of the rooms, but Jamal wouldn't reveal the
contents or his plan.

One afternoon while Judd and Nada were
exercising, Lionel took a call from Samuel.
"I have been thinking about what Dan and
Nina said before they died, and the verse you
gave me."

Lionel had almost forgotten about the
words he had handed to Samuel. It was the
strangest verse he had ever given a nonbe-
liever, but he thought it applied.

The words of Jesus were found in Luke 12.
"From now on families will be split apart,
three in favor of me, and two against—or the
other way around. There will be a division
between father and son. . . ." Lionel had
finished the note by writing, *The truth may
divide you and your father, but it's always best to
stick with the truth.*

Samuel said, "I have read that verse over
and over. I had always thought to obey my
father was the best thing I could do as a son."

"You're supposed to honor your father,"
Lionel said. "But if your dad believes some-

thing that's wrong, or asks you to do something that goes against what God wants, you have to disobey him."

"I've always believed that if I do the right things I will someday get to heaven. But I have been reading this rabbi's writings on the Internet, and I have been reading the words of Jesus in the Gospels. I don't know how to get to heaven."

"There's only one way," Lionel said.

Lionel explained that Jesus was not just a good teacher, but God in the flesh. "His mission was to live a perfect life and die as a sacrifice for your sins and mine. And he did that."

"Dan and Nina always said I could never earn my way into heaven," Samuel said.

"They were right," Lionel said. "The way to heaven is open right now. And God will show you what to do about your dad."

"Will I have to leave home if I pray this?"

"I don't know," Lionel said. "Becoming a believer doesn't make everything smooth. As a matter of fact, if your dad finds out, things will probably get worse. That's why I wrote what I did after that verse I gave you. It's better to find the truth and follow it than to live a lie."

Lionel paused. He could hear the street

sounds in the background and pictured Samuel standing at the pay phone across from his house. "Are you ready to pray?"

Samuel hesitated. "Once I do this, I cannot go back, can I?"

"Once you ask God to come into your heart, you'll never want to live any other way. I wonder every day how we're going to get home. I've been through stuff that makes me doubt I'll live another hour. But in the middle of it all, God gives me peace. I know what'll happen after I die, and that I'll be with God and my family who disappeared."

"I wish I could have that confidence," Samuel said.

"You can," Lionel said.

"Tell me again how I should pray."

"Just tell God you've done bad stuff and you're sorry. You believe that Jesus came to die for your sins and right now you accept his gift of salvation. Ask God to come into your life and make you a new person. Say you want him to save you and guide you for the rest of your life."

Lionel paused. All he could hear was the sound of the street behind Samuel. For a moment he thought the boy had left the phone off the hook and had walked away.

"Samuel?" Lionel said.

"I am here," Samuel said. "I just prayed and asked God to forgive me."

"That's great," Lionel said. "How do you feel?"

"I'm not sure," Samuel said. "Like I have finally found what I was looking for. Like Dan and Nina did not die in vain."

"I want you to do me a favor," Lionel said.

"Anything," Samuel said.

"Are there people walking on your street?"

"A few. And there are some at an outdoor café nearby."

"Get ready," Lionel said. "God has done something special to help you. Look at the people and see if any of them have a special mark on their forehead. It should look like a cross."

The phone clanked against the booth. A few seconds later, Samuel returned, out of breath. "I see someone! He just walked past."

"Go back and ask if he sees anything on your forehead," Lionel said.

Again, Samuel went away and came back overjoyed. "He called me *brother!* He said I have the mark as well, but I don't see anything."

Lionel explained the mark and that you could not see your own. "We can use this to our advantage. We know who the other believers are, but no one can see the mark except us."

Samuel was thrilled. "I want to talk to my father. I want him to have this same peace."

"But you have to be careful," Lionel said. "And you have to be prepared for your father not to accept what you've said."

Lionel told Samuel to continue reading his Bible and Tsion's Web site. Lionel couldn't wait to tell Mr. Stein and Judd what had happened.

TEN

Reunion

JUDD was elated when he heard the news about Samuel. Mr. Stein smiled broadly, then shook his head. "I'm afraid that boy is in for a difficult time if he tries to talk with his father about Christ. We should pray for him."

Judd could tell Mr. Stein was restless, but something else seemed to be bothering him. Judd brought it up one evening.

"I am concerned about Yitzhak," Mr. Stein said, "but even if he is okay, I do not think I should leave you two alone. I brought you here, and I should provide you a way home."

"Nonsense," Judd said. "We came because we wanted to."

"Still, I cannot abandon you simply because I have a wonderful opportunity."

Lionel leaned forward. "You keep talking

about God providing. Don't you think he can provide for us just as easily as he can provide for you?"

"Of course, but—"

"God will provide for us," Lionel said.

The next evening Judd took a call from Samuel. He said he had been reading Tsion's Web site as much as possible, but his father had been home and he didn't dare risk reading it then.

"I overheard a conversation with headquarters," Samuel said. "They have released all the local committee members. After the death of your friend, the GC was concerned how it would look if that information leaked to the public."

Judd felt guilty keeping the information about Mr. Stein from Samuel. Judd felt it best that Samuel not know so he wouldn't have to lie to his father.

"Won't the local committee know Mr. Stein is gone?" Judd said. "Couldn't they leak the story?"

"They were told he was banished to his homeland to face criminal charges," Samuel said.

Judd couldn't wait to see Yitzhak's face when Mr. Stein walked into the room. He asked Samuel how it felt to be a believer in Christ.

"It feels wonderful! I am learning so much in such a little time. I hope to speak with my father soon."

"Choose your time wisely," Judd said.

Vicki talked with Mark and Conrad about Janie. She was becoming increasingly difficult to work with. Vicki had threatened to withhold meals if Janie didn't pitch in, but Janie had complained about the food and said she didn't want it anyway.

"I feel responsible," Mark said. "I was the one who brought her here."

"I'm glad you did," Vicki said. "We want this place to be open to skeptics and seekers."

"We can't just kick her out," Conrad said. "She might get caught. Knowing her, she'd tell the GC about us just to get a half hour of TV privileges."

"I'd like to throw her in the tunnel and lock both doors," Vicki said.

"That would be an effective evangelism tool," Conrad said. "Convert or we'll starve you."

Vicki smiled. "Maybe we should just keep praying that God will cause her to come around."

"Any news from Judd and Lionel?" Mark said.

Vicki frowned. "They're stuck."

Judd walked beside Lionel, just behind Jamal. Mr. Stein wore a cloak over his head and held onto Jamal's arm. Judd couldn't tell what part of the Old City they were in, but he could imagine an upper room and frightened disciples waiting to be arrested by Roman guards.

They passed through a garden, then up a narrow alley. Clothes were hung out to dry on a wire strung between the buildings. The light was fading. Something about the scene filled Judd with sadness, but he couldn't figure it out. Then it came to him. *There should be children playing here, kicking a ball and laughing.* But there were no children.

Jamal cautiously led them through a doorway and up two flights of rickety stairs. He knocked twice, waited, then knocked twice again. The door creaked open, and the group was waved in quickly.

Yitzhak sat in the corner with a blanket draped over his frail shoulders. His voice was weak and he had bruises about his head. He welcomed Jamal but didn't seem to recognize Judd and Lionel.

Daniel, the emcee of the Meeting of the Witnesses, sat beside Yitzhak. About a dozen others sat at tables and on the floor.

"Who is our mystery guest?" Yitzhak said weakly.

Mr. Stein slowly removed the cloak from his head. Yitzhak's eyes filled with tears. He stood, then fell back against the wall. Mr. Stein rushed to him and embraced him.

"When we were told you had been sent home," Yitzhak said, "we feared they had killed you."

Others in the group surrounded Mr. Stein and hugged him. Some praised God in Hebrew. Others smiled and clapped. After a few minutes of conversation, Yitzhak lifted a hand.

"We have been given the task to go into the world and reap a great soul harvest," Yitzhak said. "My brother, Mitchell Stein, has asked for a time of intense study. We have prepared a place for that, as well as rest for those who have been through a difficult ordeal.

"God has delivered us from the hands of our enemies for a purpose. And we will fulfill our destiny as God's spokesmen to a lost and confused world. May he grant us the strength and the wisdom and the courage to do it."

Mr. Stein turned to Judd and Lionel with tears in his eyes. He cupped his hands around their necks and pulled them close to him.

"I feel so torn. I don't want to let you down but—"

"We understand," Lionel said. "We want you to go."

"I cannot say when we will be together again," Mr. Stein said.

Jamal stepped forward. "These are our young brothers in the faith. We will make sure they are safe."

Mr. Stein called for quiet in the room and explained what he, Judd, and Lionel had been through. "I would like to ask someone to pray for my young friends."

Yitzhak motioned the others forward. All the people in the room stretched out their hands toward Judd and Lionel, and those standing closest to them laid hands on them directly.

"Our Father," Yitzhak began, "we thank you for those who trust in you, no matter what their age. We remember the words of the apostle Paul who said, 'Don't let anyone think less of you because you are young. Be an example to all believers in what you teach, in the way you live, in your love, your faith, and your purity.' These friends have lived that verse, and we praise you for their lives."

Those touching Lionel and Judd said "Amen," "Yes, Lord," and other words Judd couldn't understand.

Yitzhak continued. "We give them to you now and ask that you would give them spiritual wisdom and understanding so that they may grow in their knowledge of you. I pray their hearts will be flooded with light so that they can understand the wonderful future you have promised to those you have called. Help them to realize what a rich and glorious inheritance you have given your people."

Judd realized Yitzhak was praying the same prayer for Lionel and him that Paul prayed in Ephesians.

Yitzhak continued. "O God, help our friends begin to understand the incredible greatness of your power. May they experience this power that raised Christ from the dead and seated him in the place of honor at your right hand in heaven. We know that Jesus is now far above any ruler or authority or power or leader or anything else in this world or in the world to come. May he be praised by all of our lives, and the lives of these two young men, until we see him coming in the clouds at the Glorious Appearing.

"We give you Judd and Lionel, O Father, and we give you our lives. Every breath we have is yours. In Jesus' name. Amen."

Lionel awoke before the others the next morning and opened Tsion's Web page. Tsion included some personal notes in his teaching for the day. He wrote about the heartbreak of losing family members and friends.

The death of Ken Ritz has gotten to him, Lionel thought.

Tsion ended his teaching with a reminder that "we are but a year and a half from what the Scriptures call the Great Tribulation. It has been hard, worse than hard, so far. We have survived the worst two years in the history of our planet, and this next year and a half will be worse. But the last three and a half years of this period will make the rest seem like a garden party."

Tsion always concluded with a word of encouragement, no matter how difficult the teaching had been. He quoted Luke 21: "'There will be signs in the sun, in the moon, and in the stars; and on the earth distress of nations, with perplexity, the sea and the waves roaring; men's hearts failing them for fear and the expectation of those things which are coming on the earth, for the powers of the heavens will be shaken. Then they will see the Son of Man coming in a cloud with power and great glory. Now when these things begin to happen, look up and lift up your heads, because your redemption draws near.'"

Lionel flipped on the television and kept the sound low. Nicolae Carpathia was still upset about the actions of Eli and Moishe. The reporter cut to Leon Fortunato at a news conference.

"His Excellency has decreed the preachers enemies of the world system and has authorized Peter the Second, supreme pontiff of Enigma Babylon One World Faith, to dispose of the criminals as he sees fit."

The response from Peter Mathews seemed almost comical to Lionel. Mathews was furious. "Oh, the problem is mine now, is it? Has His Excellency finally given authority to the person who deserves it? When the two lie dead and the rains fall again in Israel, clear, pure, refreshing water will cascade once more, and the world will know who has the true power."

Lionel thought of Vicki and his friends at the schoolhouse. It was midnight in the Midwest, and he guessed everyone was asleep as he saw the sun rise. He opened the door to the roof and walked quietly upstairs. He wondered what Mr. Stein was learning and what would happen to him and Judd.

There were no clouds in the sky. The sun was so brilliant that Lionel had to squint. He was high enough to see the gates of the Old City. The new temple gleamed brilliantly in the bright light.

Lionel closed his eyes and felt the warmth. Suddenly, he felt a chill. He opened his eyes to what looked like twilight. It was as if someone had let down the blinds on heaven. The sun was still visible in the sky, but it had faded. The temperature immediately fell.

Lionel rushed back to his computer and pulled up Tsion's message from the Meeting of the Witnesses. He found the section he was looking for and flipped his Bible open to Revelation 8:12. "Then the fourth angel blew his trumpet, and one-third of the sun was struck, and one-third of the moon, and one-third of the stars, and they became dark. And one-third of the day was dark and one-third of the night also."

Lionel shook Judd awake. "The next judgment's here!"

Judd rushed to the roof and pulled his blanket tightly around him. Jamal and his wife joined them.

"This is going to affect everything," Judd said, "not just how much light we get and how low the temperature will go. Plants are going to die. There'll be food shortages. Water lines will freeze."

"Communication lines will be affected," Jamal said. "Much of the new GC technology is solar powered."

"And transportation," Jamal's wife said gravely. "Travel will be impossible in a few days."

Jamal motioned them back inside. "It is time to answer your questions." He closed the door and sealed off the roof with heavy tape so the cold air could not get through.

Back in the living area, Jamal opened a box. "Tsion told us to prepare, and we have." Inside the box was nonperishable food. The next box contained warm clothes and blankets. "I also purchased these." Jamal unpacked several freestanding fireplaces. "I would never allow them in the building under normal circumstances, but these are not normal circumstances."

"These won't do us any good if we don't have fuel," Judd said.

"Have you seen the new Dumpsters at the back of the building?" Jamal said.

Lionel nodded. "They're huge."

"Each is locked and filled with firewood. I estimate one Dumpster could keep us warm twenty-four hours a day for up to two weeks."

"How many Dumpsters?" Judd said.

"Ten," Jamal said. "That could last us as long as five months. However, we may need to shelter others, and that means we will have to use more wood to heat the rooms."

Jamal showed them another source of heat he had invented. It used a simple exercise bicycle and a weird contraption hooked to it. "I have five of these. It will not only give us heat, but a good workout as well."

The phone rang. Nada handed the phone to Lionel. It was Samuel. The boy shivered at the phone booth. Lionel tried to calm him, but Samuel was frightened.

"This is exactly what the Bible said would happen," Lionel said. "God's trying to get people's attention again."

"My father left early this morning, before the sky darkened," Samuel said. "I want to tell him about my faith, but I'm scared. What if he kicks me out?"

"You can come here if you have to," Lionel said, "but try to wait until you think your father's ready to listen."

Judd asked for the phone, and Lionel gave it to him. "This may be your chance to tell your dad the truth. You can say Tsion predicted all this. If your father seems open, show him the passage in the Bible."

Lionel walked to the nearest window. There was a flurry of activity as Jamal and his family and the others staying with them opened boxes and prepared for the cold days ahead. Lionel looked out at the city of Jerusalem. He wondered if his friends back home had prepared. Surely people would die from this, especially those who were used to warm temperatures.

Lionel prayed for his friends and got to work.

ELEVEN

Frozen!

WHEN Vicki awoke the next morning, she pulled the covers up under her chin. The air was chilly. She was used to the sunshine waking her between six-thirty and seven. Sometimes she pulled the covers over her head to sleep a little longer.

She picked her watch up from the floor and turned it several times before she could see. It was after seven o'clock.

Strange, Vicki thought, swinging her feet from under the covers and hitting the floor. She quickly jumped back into bed. The floor was icy.

No one was up yet, so Vicki went to the computer room to read Tsion's Web site. The Internet seemed unusually slow.

Vicki blew warm air into her hands and

noticed she could see her breath. When a window popped on her screen with a news flash about the worldwide cold spell, Vicki finally realized what had happened.

She called the others together. Slowly people made their way into the room. Mark walked onto the balcony on the second floor to see the lack of sunlight, but he couldn't stand to stay outside long.

Vicki logged on to the local news. The report said a cold front had moved into Illinois in the middle of the night. Meteorologists and other weather experts tried to make sense of the situation, but all seemed stumped.

Janie shuffled into the room with a blanket draped around her. "Who turned down the heat? I'm freezing!"

"It's the judgment we told you about," Vicki said.

Janie looked at Vicki like she had two heads. "What are you talking about?"

Vicki picked up a Bible and read the passage that described the striking of the sun, moon, and stars.

"This means we need to get in gear," Mark said. He and Conrad ran to start the generator.

Vicki, Darrion, and Shelly inspected the house and decided the upstairs would be too difficult to heat. "Too much cold air coming through those old windows," Vicki said.

"We'll need to move everybody to the ground floor."

"I don't want to be cooped up down here," Janie protested.

Vicki remained firm. When it was time for lunch, the kids huddled near the computer to watch the official reaction from the Global Community.

A spokesperson for the Global Community Aeronautics and Space Administration read a prepared statement in front of reporters. The man tried to look calm and confident.

"Regarding the incident that occurred 0700 hours New Babylon time today, the GCASA is pleased to assure the public that the darkening of the skies is the result of an explainable natural phenomenon and should not be a cause of alarm. Top scientific researchers have concluded that this is a condition that should correct itself in somewhere between forty-eight and ninety-six hours."

Reporters' hands went up and several shouted questions. The man tried to calm them, then continued. "I won't be taking questions at this time. As you were told, this is a prepared statement."

"I can tell you why he's not taking questions," Mark said. "He doesn't have any answers."

The scientist continued. "This event should not affect temperatures greatly, except in the short run."

Mark snickered. "Yeah, in the short run while all of us freeze to death."

"There may be some impact on smaller solar-powered equipment such as cell phones, computers, and calculators for a few days, but there should be no measurable impact on the power reserves."

The scientist gave one theory. He said the phenomenon's probable cause was an explosion of a massive star—a supernova. "The explosion resulted in the formation of a magnetar—a supermagnetized star—that can spin at a high rate of speed, causing elements in its core to rise and become extremely magnetic."

"See," Janie said, "this is not some kind of judgment from God. They have a perfect explanation."

"It's nonsense," Conrad said. "I read about this in school. If a magnetar would have happened as close as he says, the earth would be hurtling out into space right now."

"You think you know more than this guy?" Janie said.

Mark asked them to be quiet as the scientist continued.

"The GCASA will maintain constant watch

on the situation and report significant changes. We expect things to be normal before the end of next week."

Judd wanted to watch the Global Community's coverage of the disaster, but there was too much to do. Getting heat to the rooms and opening boxes took time.

Jamal was frantic with calls from the lower apartments. Power from the Global Community was running at 50 percent strength, and the main heating unit was already struggling to pump warm air throughout the building.

"We have to make a decision," Jamal said. "There are about five hundred people living here. If the judgment continues for more than a week, some of those may die."

"We can't fit five hundred people up here," Judd said.

"But we could help some," Jamal said.

"Wait," Lionel said. "Maybe we could set up a couple of your heaters in a big room downstairs. Isn't there some kind of meeting room near the lobby?"

Jamal nodded. "Excellent idea. We could spare three of the wood-burning fireplaces and place them about the room. We would need to find ventilation, but it might work."

"And if we find other believers, we can invite them up," Judd said.

Judd and the others were exhausted by evening. They had set up a heating center in the large meeting room downstairs. The room allowed four hundred occupants, but Jamal had knocked out a wall to an adjoining room so that everyone in the building could stay warm.

Judd ate soup and watched the evening newscast. He could tell the Global Community was scrambling, and he loved it. A newscaster recapped the story and announced that a special panel would comment about the situation the following day. The panel members included famed botanist, Chaim Rosenzweig.

"That's the guy Buck, Tsion, and Chloe stayed with," Lionel said. "He's not a believer, is he?"

Jamal shook his head. "I don't think so."

"You think he'll follow the GC party line?" Judd said.

"Rosenzweig is asked to comment about everything in Israel," Jamal said. "When the disappearances occurred, he agreed with one theory the GC gave. He'll probably agree with them again."

Vicki walked outside to look at the setting sun. The gray sky hung like a blanket over the countryside. Vicki thought it looked like snow, but she knew this was nothing that could be explained by weather patterns. This was God at work.

Vicki shivered in the cold and said a prayer. She thanked God for providing them with a place to stay and enough food to keep them going. She prayed especially for Melinda, Janie, and Charlie—that their eyes would be opened to the truth. Then her thoughts turned toward Judd. She hadn't heard from him in days. She had hoped he would be on his way home, but that would be impossible now. Wherever Judd, Lionel, and Mr. Stein were, they would be stuck there until this judgment was over.

Conrad came outside and shoved his hands into his pockets. "The news is almost on. Thought you'd want to see what the GC has been advertising all day."

Vicki nodded. As they moved toward the house, Conrad stopped her. "I really respect what you've done. You've taken a lot on your shoulders. I'll do everything I can to help."

"That means a lot," Vicki said.

Janie shivered when Vicki walked in. "Close the door!"

Vicki ignored her and went to the meeting room. It was the warmest room in the house, and it felt ice-cold. Mark had made a fire in the fireplace, and most of the kids were bundled in blankets.

The program began with introductions of the various guests. Some were scientists or representatives of the Global Community, while others were authors or even entertainers.

"I don't get it," Shelly said when they introduced one guest. "She's not an astronomer—she's a singer!"

"Every time the GC wants people to buy what they're saying," Mark said, "they make it a popularity contest. As if that's what makes something true."

The host introduced Chaim Rosenzweig. The news anchor listed his many achievements, including his winning the Nobel Prize and being personal friends with His Excellency, Nicolae Carpathia.

"I wonder how many people are watching this," Darrion said.

"It's the only game in town," Conrad said. "The GC has this on every channel and all over the Net."

Melinda, Charlie, and Janie sat close to the computer screen. Vicki wondered about people who didn't know the truth. With the disappearances, the earthquake, the meteor, and poisoned water, they had to be terrified. This program was their best hope for real answers. Vicki cringed when she saw the guests.

Each participant praised the Global Community for their work and promised this was a minor, temporary condition. A woman from Global Community Power and Light said, "As alarming as the darkness is, we agree it will have a very small impact on our quality of life. The problem should correct itself in a matter of days."

When Chaim spoke, Vicki sensed something different. He made the host squirm with his first response. When he had everyone's attention he said, "I am not a religious man. A Jew by birth, of course, and proud of it. But to me it's a nationality, not a faith."

Dr. Rosenzweig talked of his former student Tsion Ben-Judah. Vicki's heart sank when Chaim referred to Tsion's belief in Jesus as "madness." When the host tried to interrupt him, Dr. Rosenzweig said, "I have earned the right to another minute or so.

"Ben-Judah was ridiculed for his belief that

scriptural prophecy would actually happen. He said an earthquake would come. It came. He said hail and rain and fire would scorch the plants. They did. He said things would fall from the sky, poisoning water, killing people, sinking ships. They fell.

"He said the sun and the moon and the stars would be stricken and that the world would be one-third darker. Well, I am finished. I don't know what to make of it except that I feel a bigger fool every day. And let me just add, I want to know what Dr. Tsion Ben-Judah says is coming next! Don't you?"

Dr. Rosenzweig quickly gave the address of Tsion's Web site. The camera panned back to the host, who was speechless.

"Go ahead now," Chaim said. "Pull the plug on me."

"I don't believe it," Conrad said. "He just gave Tsion the best publicity he's ever had!"

Vicki watched Melinda, Janie, and Charlie carefully. While the other kids cheered, they stared at the screen.

Judd couldn't believe Dr. Rosenzweig had mentioned Tsion's Web site. Though the man wasn't a believer, he had caught the Global Community off guard. Judd wondered if Chaim would suffer for his statements, or if the host of the program would be punished for not cutting Chaim off.

Judd quickly logged on and watched the number of people accessing the site swell. Lionel said, "This is the biggest Web site in the world as it is. Now he's going to get ten times the hits."

Over the next few days, people around the world tried to adjust to the cold. Many believed the GC reports that it would last about a week. But the longer the cold continued, the more things shut down. News reports from remote areas became scarce because of the energy crisis. People who had lived near the equator all their lives died from the sudden blast of arctic air. In Israel, snow fell. The only ones who didn't seem to notice the cold were Eli and Moishe. They stood in their bare feet and preached, unaffected by the temperature change.

Jamal kept a pot of boiling water going at all times. The steam helped heat the apartment. Jamal's wife had hot cups of tea and coffee to keep people warm. Because of the power shortage, they had to cut down on their computer usage.

"Will any believers die from this?" Lionel asked one day.

Jamal shrugged. "I wish I could ask Tsion all of my questions."

With the cramped quarters, Judd found himself spending more and more time with Nada. She was easy to talk with and interesting. Judd shared some of the things he had learned from Bruce and told her the stories of the Young Tribulation Force.

"Do you think I could be a member of your group?" Nada said.

Judd smiled. "I think the only requirements are that you're ready to go anywhere and do anything that God asks you to do."

Later that day, Lionel asked to talk with Judd in private. They moved to the corner of a room.

"Nada wants to know if she can be a member of the Young Trib Force," Judd said.

Lionel looked away. "That's what I want to talk to you about. Do you think it's a good idea to get close to someone like this?"

"Close?" Judd said. "Just because two people talk doesn't mean—"

"It just seems like there's more going on than that," Lionel said.

"You're crazy," Judd said. "We're just friends."

"If I'm wrong, I'll admit it," Lionel said, "but why don't you ask her?"

"I don't want to talk about it," Judd said.

The phone rang. It was Samuel. He sounded tired and scared.

"Where are you?" Judd asked.

"I finally talked with my father," Samuel said. "I followed your advice. I mentioned the possibility that Dr. Ben-Judah could be right and that we should read his Web site."

"What did your father say?" Judd said.

"He got very angry and accused me of being a traitor. I think he suspects I helped in your escape."

Judd quickly told Samuel's story to Jamal and the others.

"Tell him he can come here," Jamal said.

Judd relayed the message through the increasing static on the phone. "If your dad throws you out or you don't think you can live there anymore, we have a place for you."

Samuel thanked Judd. "I want to give it one more try. I will call you tomorrow and let you know what happened."

TWELVE

Nicolae's Bargain

WHEN Samuel didn't call the next day, Judd got worried. "We need to check on him."

Lionel didn't like the idea. "What if it's a trap?"

"We can't abandon him," Judd said.

"But if we go, they might be waiting for us," Lionel said.

"I'll go," Nada said. "They won't expect a girl."

"No way your dad will go for it," Judd said.

"We don't have to tell him."

Lionel shook his head. "Sounds too risky."

Nada looked at Judd. "You said a member of the Young Trib Force needs to be ready to do anything and go anywhere God wants. I'm ready."

Jamal walked into the room, and Judd took Nada aside. "Lionel thinks there's something going on between you and me. I told him we were just friends."

Nada looked away, then turned to Judd and smiled. "Your friend has quite an imagination. It has been a long time since I have had someone my own age to talk with. If I gave the wrong impression, I'm sorry."

"Now, about you going to see Samuel—"

Nada waved him off. "It's settled. I'm going."

Before the change in the weather, Vicki had hoped to make the school a training ground for the Young Trib Force. But when the sun, moon, and stars went dark, Vicki just wanted to keep all the believers and Melinda, Charlie, and Janie warm and alive. When she postponed classes again, the kids understood, but were unhappy. They knew they couldn't learn much with the frigid temperatures. But Janie had clapped when she heard the news. "I didn't want to learn that stuff anyway," she said.

The kids watched news reports from different parts of the world. The Midwest looked like Alaska in the dead of winter. The first casualties in Chicago were at the zoos. Both the Lincoln Park Zoo and Brookfield Zoo reported all animals dead except penguins and polar bears. But things got worse. Chicago, New York, and Los Angeles estimated that hundreds of homeless people had frozen to death in the first week. Before the disappearances, many of the shelters had been staffed by Christians. Those people were gone now.

Popular resorts along warm beaches closed. Ice formed along the shoreline. As the icy weather took its toll, the Global Community was forced to change its predictions about how long the cold spell would last. Forecasts of a few days turned into a few weeks, and Global Community spokespersons turned the blame on Rabbi Ben-Judah and his followers. Peter the Second called the preaching of Eli and Moishe "black magic." Within a few weeks the estimates of deaths related to the weird weather was in the hundreds of thousands.

Nicolae Carpathia finally appeared before the world in a bare television studio in New Babylon. The kids watched, huddled together, as Carpathia clapped his mittens and praised the loyalty and courage of each citizen.

"I come to you at this hour to announce

my plan to personally visit the two preachers at the Wailing Wall," Carpathia said. "They must be forced to admit they are behind this assault on our new way of life."

"I can't believe he's actually going to face them," Shelly said.

"At least he admits they have power," Mark said.

Carpathia said he would bargain with Eli and Moishe in hopes of ending this latest affliction. "I shall make this pilgrimage tomorrow, and it will be carried live. Take heart, my beloved ones. I believe the end of this nightmare is in sight."

Judd knew Jamal would be enraged if he heard of Nada's plan to visit Samuel. He fought with Lionel about what to do. If he drove Nada like she had asked him, Jamal would be upset. If he told Jamal of the plan, Nada would never forgive him. Finally, his commitment to Nada won out. They made plans to secretly take Jamal's car the next afternoon as the world watched Nicolae Carpathia face Eli and Moishe.

Judd hadn't ventured out of the apartment building since the judgment had begun. He was shocked at what he saw. The wind swept along in a howling blizzard. No one was on the street.

Jamal's car was kept in the bowels of the garage in an area sheltered from the cold. It took Judd a half hour to get it started. "If this thing stops on us, we're in serious trouble."

Even with three layers of clothes on, Judd was so cold he could hardly make it back inside to get Nada and return to the car. Snow blew through the garage and piled up in the corner. Breathing was difficult in the extreme cold. Judd felt his nostrils freezing, and he had to shield his eyes from the icy wind. "We can still turn back," Judd said as he got in the car. "Your dad will never know."

Nada got in and wrapped her arms around her knees. "Just drive."

Vicki and the others were up early to watch the coverage of Nicolae Carpathia on the Net. Conrad, who had been obsessed with opening the safe, reported that running the generator twenty-four hours a day had used up more gasoline than they had planned. "I think we should turn it off during the day and keep it going at night."

Vicki ran the idea past Mark.

"We can burn wood during the day and

use the generator to heat the schoolhouse at night," Mark said. "I'm for it."

Conrad switched the computer to battery power. The Global Community announcers explained that Nicolae Carpathia was in Israel, ready to bargain with the two witnesses. A message popped up on the computer that the battery was going dead.

"Already?" Mark said.

"I don't want to miss any of this," Conrad said. "I'll start the generator again."

The kids watched Carpathia approach the fence where the witnesses sat. The announcers fell silent.

"I bring you cordial greetings from the Global Community," Carpathia said, speaking to Eli and Moishe. "I assume, because of your powers, that you knew I was coming."

As Moishe began to answer, an E-mail message popped up on the screen.

"Great timing," Janie said sarcastically.

Darrion moved closer. "Looks like it's from that GC guy, Carl."

"Get out of the way; I want to see this," Janie said.

Suddenly the computer went blank. The kids groaned in unison.

"Battery's dead," Mark said.

"Did you see the message?" Vicki said.

Mark shook his head. "I'll go see what's keeping Conrad—"

Conrad stood in the doorway, his face ashen. "The generator won't work now. Gas line must have immediately frozen when I turned it off a few minutes ago."

"We're dead," Janie said.

Lionel promised Judd and Nada he would cover for them. When Jamal asked about them, Lionel pretended he didn't hear and turned up the volume on the television. Nicolae Carpathia went back and forth with the witnesses, who seemed not to want to let the potentate get the upper hand.

"I am seeking your help as men who claim to speak for God," Carpathia said. "If this is of God, then I plead with you to help me come to some arrangement, an agreement, a compromise, if you will."

"Your quarrel is not with us."

"Well, all right, I understand that, but if you have access to him—"

"Your quarrel is not w—"

"I appreciate that point! I am asking—"

Moishe's voice blared through the speakers. "You would dare wag your tongue at the chosen ones of almighty God?"

"I apologize. I—"

"You who boasted that we would die before the due time?"

"Granted, I concede that I—"

"You who denies the one true God, the God of Abraham, Isaac, and Jacob?"

Carpathia sputtered something about tolerance. Moishe countered with, "There is one God and one mediator between God and man, the man Christ Jesus."

A few minutes later the witnesses repeated, "Your quarrel is not with us," and turned away from Carpathia.

Nicolae looked confused. "So, that is it, then? Before the eyes of the world, you refuse to talk? All I get is that my quarrel is not with you? With whom, then, is it? All right, fine!"

"What do you think he'll do now?" Lionel said.

"Watch," Jamal said.

Carpathia moved close to the main camera and spoke precisely, his face clearly freezing in the cold. Lionel thought he looked desperate.

"Upon further review," Carpathia said, "the death of the Global Community guard at the Meeting of the Witnesses was not the responsibility of any of the witnesses. The man killed by GC troops at the airport was not a terrorist. As of this moment, no one who agrees with Dr. Ben-Judah and his teachings is considered a fugitive or an enemy of the Global Community. All citizens are equally free to travel and live their lives in a spirit of liberty.

"I do not know with whom I am or should be talking, but I stand willing to do whatever it takes to end this plague of darkness."

The camera followed Carpathia as he turned on his heel, sarcastically saluted the two witnesses, and reboarded the motor coach. Before the news anchors could speak, the witnesses said together, "Woe, woe, woe unto all who fail to look up and lift up your heads!"

Judd drove by Samuel's house. He kept moving another block and turned into an alley. "Before you go, tell me what you're going to do."

"I'm going to see if he's okay. If he's not, I'll bring him here."

"Just like that?"

"Just like that."

Nada opened the door to get out, and a blast of cold air hit Judd in the face. It took his breath away. Nada quickly closed the door again, took a deep breath, and then finally got out. Judd watched her run from the car, her hand over her face. She was either the bravest girl he knew or the most foolish.

Nada made it to the house and went straight to the front door. Judd couldn't imagine what she would say or do. If Mr. Goldberg was there . . .

The door opened. Judd stretched to see who it was. Suddenly, a hand grabbed Nada's arm and pulled her inside.

Vicki knew they were in trouble. Until now the cold had made life difficult. Some of the food had frozen. It was difficult sleeping when you could see your breath. But now their source of power was gone and, with it, their best source of heat.

Vicki sent the kids into emergency mode. While Conrad and Mark worked desperately at the generator, Vicki and the others brought in more firewood and stacked it in the meeting room. The kids moved their mattresses and sleeping bags into the room. Janie complained and blamed Conrad for their problems, but Vicki told her to keep quiet.

Shelly returned from the storage area, her

teeth chattering. She held up three bottles of water, all frozen solid.

"Put it by the fire," Vicki said. "We'll ration it until we can thaw some more."

Conrad and Mark came back. Conrad volunteered to keep the fire going all night.

"I don't know if I trust him," Janie said. "You see what he did to the generator!"

"I've had enough out of you," Mark yelled. "If you think you can survive without us—"

Vicki held up a hand. "Settle down. Let's just see if we can make it through tonight."

Vicki and a few others held hands and prayed before they went to sleep that night. "God, you were able to stop the lions from eating Daniel," Mark prayed. "You saved Noah from the water that flooded the world. Now we're asking for another miracle. Help us figure out a way to keep warm during this judgment."

When they finished praying, Melinda scooted her sleeping bag next to Vicki.

"Are we going to die?" Melinda whispered.

ABOUT THE AUTHORS

Jerry B. Jenkins (www.jerryjenkins.com) is the writer of the Left Behind series. He is author of more than one hundred books, of which eleven have reached the *New York Times* best-seller list. Former vice president for publishing for the Moody Bible Institute of Chicago, he also served many years as editor of *Moody* magazine and is now Moody's writer-at-large.

His writing has appeared in publications as varied as *Reader's Digest, Parade,* in-flight magazines, and many Christian periodicals. He has written books in four genres: biography, marriage and family, fiction for children, and fiction for adults.

Jenkins's biographies include books with Hank Aaron, Bill Gaither, Luis Palau, Walter Payton, Orel Hershiser, Nolan Ryan, Brett Butler, and Billy Graham, among many others.

Eight of his apocalyptic novels—*Left Behind, Tribulation Force, Nicolae, Soul Harvest, Apollyon, Assassins, The Indwelling,* and *The Mark*—have appeared on the Christian Booksellers Association's best-selling fiction list and the *Publishers Weekly* religion best-seller list. *Left Behind* was nominated for Book of the Year by the Evangelical Christian Publishers Association in 1997, 1998, 1999, and 2000. *The Indwelling* was number one on the *New York Times* best-seller list for four consecutive weeks.

As a marriage and family author and speaker, Jenkins has been a frequent guest on Dr. James Dobson's *Focus on the Family* radio program.

Jerry is also the writer of the nationally syndicated sports story comic strip *Gil Thorp,* distributed to newspapers across the United States by Tribune Media Services.

Jerry and his wife, Dianna, live in Colorado.

Dr. Tim LaHaye (www.timlahaye.com), who conceived the idea of fictionalizing an account of the Rapture and the Tribulation, is a noted author, minister, and nationally recognized speaker on Bible prophecy. He is the founder of both Tim LaHaye Ministries and The Pre-Trib Research Center. Presently Dr. LaHaye speaks at many of the major Bible prophecy conferences in the U.S. and Canada, where his nine current prophecy books are very popular.

Dr. LaHaye holds a doctor of ministry degree from Western Theological Seminary and the doctor of literature degree from Liberty University. For twenty-five years he pastored one of the nation's outstanding churches in San Diego, which grew to three locations. It was during that time that he founded two accredited Christian high schools, a Christian school system of ten schools, and Christian Heritage College.

Dr. LaHaye has written over forty books, with over 30 million copies in print in thirty-three languages. He has written books on a wide variety of subjects, such as family life, temperaments, and Bible prophecy. His current fiction works, written with Jerry Jenkins—*Left Behind, Tribulation Force, Nicolae, Soul Harvest, Apollyon, Assassins, The Indwelling,* and *The Mark*—have all reached number one on the Christian best-seller charts. Other works by Dr. LaHaye are *Spirit-Controlled Temperament; How to Be Happy Though Married; Revelation Unveiled; Understanding the Last Days; Rapture under Attack; Are We Living in the End Times?;* and the youth fiction series Left Behind: The Kids.

He is the father of four grown children and grandfather of nine. Snow skiing, waterskiing, motorcycling, golfing, vacationing with family, and jogging are among his leisure activities.

—

The Future Is Clear

Check out the exciting Left Behind: The Kids series

BOOKS #19 AND #20 COMING SOON!